'Re

It wa... still heard ... heard in the memories ... every night.

'Bo?'

He was dressed in battered jeans and an open-neck white shirt, sleeves rolled up to reveal tanned forearms. He was here, all six-foot-something of pure, angry male. He got up slowly and she saw that his eyes were slate-grey and as hard.

'What did you just say?'

What *had* she just said? She was so flabbergasted by his presence that she couldn't remember… Oh, hell. Pregnant. His baby.

Oh, heavens, why did these things keep happening to her? Remy bit her bottom lip and folded her arms across her chest, thinking about damage control. 'Um…obviously I didn't mean to tell you like that…'

'You're pregnant?' Bo shouted, and she winced as his words bounced off the walls.

'Yes.'

Was it hot in here? she wondered as the floor rose and fell. Along with heat there was suddenly no air. Instinctively she reached out her hand and grabbed the edge of the bar to keep herself from falling over. ...he saw dots behind her eyes, felt the blackness ...ing closer.

...t thing she heard before crumpling to the floor ...mused comment. 'Well, now, isn't this

Joss Wood wrote her first book at the age of eight and has never really stopped writing. Her passion for putting letters on a blank screen is matched only by her love of books and travelling—especially to the wild places of Southern Africa—and possibly by her hatred of ironing and making school lunches.

Fuelled by coffee, when she's not writing or being a hands-on mum, Joss—with her background in business and marketing—works for a non-profit organisation to promote the local economic development and collective business interests of the area where she resides. Happily and chaotically surrounded by books, family and friends, she lives in KwaZulu-Natal, South Africa, with her husband, children and their many pets.

Books by Joss Wood

The Last Guy She Should Call
Flirting with the Forbidden
More Than a Fling
The Honeymoon Arrangement
Your Bed or Mine?

**Visit the Author Profile page at
millsandboon.co.uk for more titles**

ONE NIGHT,
TWO CONSEQUENCES

BY
JOSS WOOD

MILLS
BOON

Published in Great Britain 2015
by Mills & Boon, an imprint of Harlequin (UK) Limited,
Eton House, 18-24 Paradise Road, Richmond, Surrey, TW9 1SR

© 2015 Joss Wood

ISBN: 978-0-263-24892-0

Printed and bound in Spain
by CPI, Barcelona

ONE NIGHT, TWO CONSEQUENCES

I really believe that editors make books better—especially my books!—and I've been really lucky to work with some wonderfully talented people. So this book is dedicated to Flo (who taught me so much), to Laurie (who loved this book from the start), and to Charlotte (who now has the unenviable task of keeping me on the straight and narrow). Thank you for believing in me and my books and for loving my characters and the complicated situations I place them in.

CHAPTER ONE

REMY DRAYCOTT LOOKED at the open brochure in front of her as she sipped her glass of Belleaire Chardonnay. So this was the town of Bellevue, she thought, looking across the swish wine bar through the floor-to-ceiling windows onto the main street of the town. Cosmopolitan, sophisticated, quietly rich, it had an air of European elegance.

She liked it. A lot.

From what she'd seen so far on her brief tour of the towns of the Napa Valley, Bellevue—right at the north end of the valley—seemed to be a mixture of the best of the rest. It had take-your-breath-away views of the Palisade Mountains, a smidgeon of the old-world charm of Calistoga, a little of the casual elegance of St Helena and, if she had to judge by the superb gourmet burger she'd eaten for lunch at the glossy diner down the street, the same passion for food as Yountsville.

It was a pity she was only passing through… The town was begging for her to stay a little longer, explore a little more.

No, she couldn't, she thought, pushing temptation away. For the first time in—well, years, she actually had a deadline to be in a place at a specific time. And the reminder of why she had to be in Portland in three days' time had her throwing back the rest of her wine and signalling the barman for a refill.

In seventy-two hours, give or take, her mother was due to give birth to her half-sibling and Remy had promised to be there. Not in the hospital waiting room or waiting at home, like a normal person, but in the delivery room itself. With her mum—*obviously*—her grandmother, *and* her brand-new stepdad, who was just seven years old than herself.

Remy lifted her glass to her lips. She was amazed and terrified and confused about the entire situation.

Amazed that after a lifetime of being a single parent—well, that wasn't entirely true... Grandma Rosie had been her other parent in every way that counted—her intense, brilliant and fiercely feminist mother had settled down with a high school sports coach. Terrified for her because she was, in medical terms, an elderly mother—which essentially meant that a lot more could go wrong in a forty-four-year-old body than in a seventeen-year-old one. And confused because... Well, there was more than a quarter of a century's gap between her and her nearly here sibling.

Twenty-seven years... That was more than confusing—that was a tad bizarre.

It was all very weird and unsettling. Remy desperately hoped that Jan would take a different approach to raising this child than she had to her. Dear God, she could only pray. Just be *normal*, she told her still baking sibling. Normal would be perfect.

Remy felt the mood in the wine bar shift, felt the energy change. Grateful to be distracted from her thoughts, she turned her head to look at the new arrival into the elegant space. The man had stopped to talk to a couple sitting at a table close to the front door. His back was to her, so she admired the broad shoulders the white dress shirt covered, and the spectacular butt beneath the tailored, expensive black suit pants.

Finished with that conversation, he moved on to the next

table, shaking hands and kissing cheeks, and Remy waited for him to turn around so that she could see his face. She rested her chin in the palm of her hand—at ease, as always, with flying solo.

In the corner a short brunette strummed a guitar and crooned into a microphone, while a group of women her age sat in a booth, laughing raucously and slamming tequilas. Groups of people were gathered around the horseshoe-shaped bar, and Remy couldn't help noticing the interested and predatory female eyes tracking Hot and Sexy's progress to the bar. In a room brimming with handsome and successful men he had the ability to capture a lot of attention without doing much at all.

He eventually made it to the general vicinity of where she was sitting and Remy could—finally!—see that face up close and personal: wavy dark brown hair, almost black, a long nose, and deep-set, mysterious eyes. Strong jaw, sexy mouth.

Oh, yeah. Very hot. Incredibly sexy.

Remy tipped her head as he was pulled into yet another conversation and noticed that while he didn't seem to say much when he did people listened. *Really* listened. Even in silence he exuded confidence and control. More than his face or his body—both of which were panty-droppingly attractive—it was that control and confidence that intrigued her. Alpha male, she decided quickly: powerful, wealthy, in charge.

She'd known many alpha men. They had littered the offices, bars and pavements of New York. 'Arrogant' and 'entitled' hadn't turned her head for a long, long time. He did. And she had to wonder why. Something about him made her lady bits quiver—and quivering was a *not* a good thing. Not good at all.

She was passing through Bellevue and she didn't need any distractions. This man, she realised instinctively, was the type who women made themselves look silly over, changed their plans for, embarrassed themselves with.

Remy was too smart to do any of the above.

Too smart, period.

Bo Tessier had noticed her as soon as he'd pushed through the glass doors to his family's wine-tasting bar in the heart of Bellevue town—a venue that both locals and tourists flocked to for their evening entertainment. Her elbow was propped on the bar and her hand held up her head. Her hair was a long fall of rich brown messy, loose curls, shot through with chestnut streaks too subtle to have come out of a salon. She had sculpted cheekbones, a stubborn chin, and a body that was long and lean—almost scrawny.

'You heard that Bella passed away?'

He pulled his attention away from the beauty at the bar and looked down at the expectant faces at the table he was standing next to. He'd been answering the same question all day. Yes, of course he'd heard that Bella Abram, his neighbour and owner of Bella's Folly—a Queen Anne mansion on five acres, bordering the east side of Bel-leaire—had passed away in her sleep the night before last.

'We're wondering who will inherit. Bella was quite well off.'

And there was the other comment he'd been hearing all day.

As for the heirs—who knew? Bella had kept the valley entertained with her many torrid affairs, but she'd never married, and since as far as anyone knew she was the only child of only children...dead end. When her heir was identified he'd be first in line with an offer to purchase. He could do without her monstrosity of a house, filled with rubbish, but he wanted that land. More land meant more vines, and there would be space for tunnels to grow organic exotic fruits and vegetables to supply their restaurants—and others in the area.

He was very aware that the land, being on the main tourist route leading into town from the more southerly towns in the Napa Valley, was also a prime spot to be developed. Belleaire did *not* need a housing estate or a golf course or a shopping mall on its doorstep. He couldn't think of anything worse.

Extricating himself from the conversation, he moved towards the busy bar as a tourist group seated in a circle rose and, gathering their jackets and bags, drifted towards the exit. Bo stepped up to the bar and raked his hand through his hair.

'Your usual, sir?' the barman asked, and Bo nodded.

The barman scuttled across the area behind the bar and Bo winced when an expensive bottle of whiskey nearly slipped from his hand. Resisting the urge to climb over the bar and pour his own drink—he'd worked behind this bar during his college years—he drummed his fingers against the surface before abruptly stopping when he recalled his sister Ginny's words.

'You intimidate the hell out of our staff, Bo. You're so distant, so unapproachable. Loosen up, smile at them occasionally. Crack a joke, compliment them.'

Years ago—before he'd lost Ana and long before he'd assumed the enormous responsibilities of running the Belleaire Group—he would have found that easier to do. These days he didn't have the time or the energy or the inclination to soft-soap people into doing their jobs.

Communication was not his strong point—as Ginny frequently reminded him.

'You can only take strong and silent so far, brother darling. No man is an island and all that…'

Bo gave a mental shrug. It worked for him, and since he worked crazy hours running their multimillion-dollar group of companies, comprising vineyards, a winery, farms, a hotel, restaurants and more than a few wine bars, he didn't see the point in fixing what wasn't broken.

Bo lifted the glass of whiskey on ice and closed his eyes as the first sip slid easily down his throat. His business might be built on wine, but there was nothing like a good shot of Irish whiskey to soothe.

Looking across the bar, he caught the eye of the barman again. 'Has my cousin been in?'

'Eli has come and gone, sir. He waited for you, but said to tell you that he'd catch up with you in the morning.'

Out of the corner of his eye he saw the woman's head lift, knew that she was listening to their conversation. He felt her eyes on his face, sensed her interest. He didn't mind—hell, she was gorgeous.

But many, *many* gorgeous women strolled in and out of this wine bar, through the tasting rooms back at the vineyard, through their restaurant, their art gallery, hotel…his office, his life. He never picked up random women. If he required female company—he was only thirty-five and he frequently did—he had a couple of women on speed dial. Women he knew, liked, was comfortable with. Women who understood that he only wanted a couple of hours' strings-free fun.

Bo placed his forearms on the bar and looked at his foot resting on the gold rail, resisting the temptation to look her way and initiate conversation. He should be heading back to the estate, to the first of the four luxury houses they'd had built when they'd decided to turn the Belleaire mansion and family home into a boutique hotel. The houses were tucked into the east end of the estate, beyond the vineyards, and were far enough away from each other so that he didn't feel as if he was living in his sister's or his cousin's pockets. The fourth house, smaller than the rest, they kept for visiting family and friends.

He had a full day tomorrow, a crazy week ahead, and he was nuts to be even *considering* chatting up this beauty with shadows under her eyes. He knew instinctively that she wasn't his type. He liked women like himself: cool, collected, calm. He could tell from the short sundress she wore with kick-ass cowboy boots, from her curly down-to-the-waist hair and make-up-free face, that this woman was a free spirit.

He always ran as far and as fast as he could away from free spirits, adventurers, women who marched to the beat of their own drum. He preferred women who were un-complicated, undemanding, easy-going. Calm… He really liked calm.

He just knew that this woman was anything but…

So toss back your whiskey and get out of here, Tessier. And there's no point in running pickup lines through your head. You are not going to use them on her or anybody else.

Smart, very successful—rich, if she had to judge by his subdued designer threads—and a little or a lot lost, Remy thought. His broad shoulders looked tight and his thumb tapping against his tumbler suggested tension. His hair held the furrows of frustrated fingers raking through it.

She recognised stress when she saw it—after all, she'd once been the living, breathing embodiment of it—and she sympathised. He needed more than one hastily thrown back whiskey and some conversation. He needed to relax, to laugh, and probably a healthy bout of really good sex.

She could help with one and two, and she couldn't em-phatically state that three was out of the question. She was *that* attracted to him…

Here's hoping you have a sense of humour, cutie, be-cause if you don't I'm about to fall flat on my face…

'You are just the way I like my coffee. Tall, dark and strong.'

He half turned towards her and she sucked in her breath at her first proper look at his eyes, which were gunmetal-grey, framed by dark, spiky lashes.

His straight, dark eyebrows pulled together. 'Excuse me?'

Remy made a clucking noise and pretended to think. 'Didn't work? Well, what about this...? I've been looking for a man with a VCR and I've finally found the perfect one... That's a Very Cute Rear, by the way.'

He rolled his eyes but she saw humour flash in them. *Thank God.*

His strong face remained impassive, and if it hadn't been for that flicker of fun she'd noticed she would have run for the hills.

'Seriously?'

Remy flashed her naughtiest grin. 'Really cheesy, huh?'

That sexy mouth tipped up just a little at the corners. 'Very.'

'Okay—last one. Aren't you the guy who's going to buy me my next drink?'

He stared at her for a moment, before releasing a smile which took him from cool and remote to vaguely accessible.

Oh, cutie, you definitely need to smile a lot more.

'Not great, but tolerable.'

His voice was low, melodious, and as smooth as the expensive whiskey he was drinking, she thought as he turned away to order her a drink. Then he took the vacant seat next to her and, as she'd expected, blinked when he noticed her eyes. Instead of commenting on the pale golden colour, as so many people did, he just crossed his arms, big biceps pulling the sleeves of his dress shirt tight across his arms. She longed to loosen that perfectly knotted red tie, to undo the top button of that blindingly white shirt. She wondered what he would look like in lived-in jeans and a T-shirt…how he looked naked. Fantastic, she decided.

'So, do those dreadful pickup lines usually work for you?' he asked, his eyes unreadable again.

'You bought me a drink, didn't you?' Remy pointed out.

'This is true.' He pushed the glass of wine in her direction. 'Got any others?'

'Pickup lines? Sure.'

'Hit me.'

'They *are* pretty dreadful,' she warned him, her expression inviting him to flirt a little, laugh a lot.

'I don't know…the VCR one was dated *and* dreadful.'

Remy tapped her finger against the bar and pretended to think. 'Okay, what about…your body is a wonderland and I want to be Alice?'

He groaned.

'Could you please step away from the bar? You're melting all the ice?'

There was that smile again.

'Are you a dictionary? Because you just gave me the definition of gorgeous?'

Yeah, the smile's growing bigger. C'mon, I know it's in there somewhere.

'You're so hot a firefighter couldn't put you out.'

His unexpected laughter rumbled over her and Remy couldn't help her shiver, which was quickly followed by heat flowing through her veins. She'd got him to smile properly, to laugh. She felt as if she'd won a seriously important prize.

She sent him another dazzling smile. 'I'm Remy.'

'Robert, but most people call me Bo.'

Robert was too uptight, too formal, Remy thought as she took a sip of her wine, but she supposed it suited his cool, calm, Lord of the Manor attitude. 'Bo' suited the laughing man she'd seen behind the stick-up-his-ass façade.

And she really found *that* man far too attractive.

This is a good time to get up and leave, Draycott. Before you do something really stupid like inviting him to inspect your panties—which just happen to be red and barely there. Take your reality pill, honey. Remember the last time you had sex? Which happened to be your first and only one-night stand? Two years ago? It was so unfulfilling that you swore you'd never do it again... Is this ringing any bells yet?

It was, but she really, *really* didn't want to listen to Sensible Remy. She wasn't any fun...

'How long are you staying in Bellevue?' he asked, distracting her from her crazy thoughts.

Remy looked at the functional, no-frills watch on her wrist. 'Ten hours or so? I'm hitting the road at first light. Do you live in the area?'

He nodded. 'Are you travelling alone?'

She knew that he was fishing—could see the attraction she felt echoed in his eyes. 'Yep, just me.'

'It's a nice holiday...touring the wine country,' he replied, his tone so bland that she wondered if she was perhaps reading him wrong.

Then his hand moved across the bar and his thumb stroked over the pulse-point of her wrist, which instantly bolted at his touch.

Holy hell, she was playing with fire, she thought, staring at his strong, broad hand on her pale wrist. Unable to pull away from his touch, so simple and so devastating, she used her other hand to pick up her wine glass and lubricate her mouth.

'So, how has your trip been so far?'

Same voice, but his eyes were on her mouth and the gunmetal-grey had turned smoky with passion. How could he keep his voice so smooth while she was a maelstrom of nerves and lust and attraction? *Kiss me, already*, she wanted to beg.

No begging allowed, Sensible Remy whispered in her ear.

'Oh, I'm not on holiday… I'm a professional vagrant.' That sounded better—a little breathy but there had been words in a sentence. Pretty impressive, really.

His thumb on her wrist stopped. *Noooo!*

'Want to explain that?' he asked.

She couldn't. All she could think about was the effect he was having on her and her desire to get him naked, to have her hands on that warm, muscled, masculine flesh. There was no way to verbalise that three years ago she'd lived in New York, that her doctorate in computer science had landed her the position of youngest Chief Information Officer of a Fortune 500 company. *Ever.*

She'd had an apartment in Manhattan, worked eighty-hour weeks, had an ulcer the size of a fist and had been prone to panic attacks. She'd been discontented, unhappy, unfulfilled. Bitchy, demanding, impatient. She could never tell him that it had taken her landing up in hospital to re-alise that she was working herself to death. And for what? A fat pay cheque and her mother's approval?

Could he even *begin* to understand why she'd given up everything because she hadn't liked what she'd been doing or who she'd been doing it for? That she'd run? To Europe, and then Africa, Asia? And when she hadn't found what she was looking for in foreign places—that nebulous, inde-finable something that would make her life make sense—she'd come home to see if she could find it by travelling through her own country.

Seeing that he was still waiting for an answer, she shrugged and bit the inside of her lip. 'I've been travel-ling for a long time.'

'Why?'

She tipped her head and shoved her tongue in her cheek. 'I'm trying to *find* myself—to work out why I *do* the things I do and *make* the choices I make.'

His lips quirked at her dramatic tone. 'Any luck with that?'

'Absolutely none,' Remy replied in a mournful voice. And even while she was mocking herself she silently admitted that she was starting to become slightly concerned that she never would.

'And how do you support yourself and your gas habit?'

That amazing thumb had resumed its rhythm on her wrist. She could no more pull her hand away than she could adjust the temperature of the sun.

Savings, investments, property... She'd worked so hard that she'd never had time to spend any of her ridiculously huge salary. She earned enough in interest and dividends and rental, and from the occasional virtual consulting job she took, to allow her to keep travelling for a long, long time. If she was really lucky she would find whatever it was that she was looking for soon—in Portland, maybe, or in the next town she visited.

'When I need to I find work.' There were always IT consulting projects popping into her inbox—some of which she took on, if they were interesting enough.

'Doing...?'

'This and that... I'm a hell of a cook—and, for the record, a really bad waitress.'

He laughed again and she felt her womb contract. Why was getting this hard-eyed, hard-bodied man to laugh such a kick? Such an incredible turn-on?

'Good to know.'

'So...what do *you* do?'

Bo lifted his eyebrows. 'What do you *think* I do?'

The corners of his mouth lifted in a sexy little smile.

Was he flirting? He was so contained that she couldn't be sure, but she'd give him the benefit of the doubt.

'I'll play that game. Well, you look marginally intelligent,' she teased. 'Accountant?'

Bo pulled a face. 'Ugh!'

She pulled a face too. 'Lawyer?'

'Double *ugh*!'

She tapped her finger against her lip. 'So, not an accountant or a lawyer? I'd still say that you're in management.'

'Yeah.'

And she just knew that he was the top branch of a very tall tree. She couldn't imagine him taking orders from anyone. He was too controlled, too alpha...not her type at all. As a long-term prospect, she clarified. Along with her career she'd also given up on love and her dreams of happy-ever-after with a nice man followed by a couple of kids. She'd finally—*finally!*—learnt that, despite what people said, love, trust and approval were conditional— very much dependent on what she delivered.

So three years and two months ago she'd stopped playing that game, and she now kept any new relationships simple. Most of them were transient and fleeting anyway, due to the fact that she was constantly on the move.

And this was pure sexual heat shimmering between her and Bo: passion, lust and incredible chemistry.

Remy lifted her head from watching his thumb on her wrist—so fascinating, so thrilling!—and her eyes slammed into his. She swallowed at the heat and passion rolling through them and sighed when Bo lifted his hand and that magical thumb brushed her full bottom lip.

'So sexy,' he muttered as his other hand gripped her thigh.

Remy looked down at his hand and could easily imagine those tanned fingers on her breast, that wide hand sliding over her hip, under her bottom, lifting her to him…

Then he leaned forward and his mouth touched hers… warm, wonderful. Remy, shocked and surprised and utterly turned on, had to grab at his biceps to keep from falling off her stool. Bo steadied her by holding her waist, and she could feel the ridges of his fingers through her thin cotton dress.

Remy held on to his wrists and, wanting more of his deliciousness, pressed her mouth back onto his. He tasted like whiskey and breath mints and his lips were a surprise. Warm, firm, dry… *Confident*. That word again. What *he* was to his core and what *she* only had a glossy, thin layer of…

His hand moved to her spine, kneading as he worked his way up to her bare shoulders, moved around to touch her face. His thumb skated over her cheekbone as he deepened the kiss, his tongue sliding into her mouth.

Remy's eyes flew open at the bolt of lust that spiked through her. Where had *that* come from? She couldn't remember when last she'd been kissed with such mastery, such complete and utter self-assurance.

She wanted more of this—more of him. Now. Tonight. One night of passion with a man she knew would rock her world.

Grabbing every last bit of courage she had, she made herself pull back from him, determined to be sensible just for a minute.

'This sounds like an extraordinarily personal question, and I know you can lie when you answer but I hope you don't. Are you married? Involved?'

Apart from those hot, tumultuous eyes, he looked as calm and collected as before. Keeping his eyes locked on hers, he drained his drink. 'No.'

'Good.' Remy nodded. 'It's one of my little rules.' She

shrugged a slim shoulder and forced herself to say the words. 'Been tested lately?'

Bo remained unruffled. 'Yep. I'm good.'

'Me too, but I'd still expect you to use a condom.'

'Noted.'

'Okay, then.'

Remy, hoping, praying, that she wasn't making the biggest mistake of her life, stood up and draped her black leather bag over her slim shoulder. She was as nervous as hell—couldn't believe that she'd had the...well, the courage to do this. Knowing that laughter would loosen the tension between them, she deliberately looked down at his feet before flashing him a naughty grin.

'You know what they say about men with big feet. Want to prove that to me?'

His shout of laughter had more than a few customers looking their way.

Yeah, laugh, cutie, Remy thought as they left the bar. *You sound amazing.*

'You okay?'

Bo's voice rumbled across her skin and Remy nodded, rubbing her head against his shoulder.

'Wonderful, thanks.'

And she genuinely was. Sleeping with Bo was nothing like the last one-night stand she'd had, and she was thrilled that it was so much more. There were no regrets this time—no feelings of guilt, no resentment at not being satisfied.

She felt relaxed and calm and, weirdly, *safe*.

She'd hit the one-night stand jackpot, Remy thought on an internal smile. Very good-looking, and his body, under those sharp threads, was droolworthy. Long, lean muscles, ripped abs, broad shoulders... And he smelled divine.

He was the best lover she'd ever had by a million miles.

Sex with Bo had been fun and, strangely for an ONS, a little romantic. That had never happened to her before. With
all her previous lovers her mind, ever analytical, had always ruled and she'd never allowed herself to fall into that
space where she stopped thinking and just enjoyed. But instead of the fast and furious she'd expected, Bo had spent
long, luscious minutes worshipping her body, allowing her
to do the same to him. It had made what should have been
a quick encounter deeper, more personal…softer.

Why was it that the one man who'd managed to show
her how sex should be, who had been able to satisfy her
beyond anything she'd believed possible, was the man she'd
never see again?

Remy watched as Bo raised his wrist and looked at the
bright dial of his watch, the roman numerals visible in the
nearly dark room. This was it. In fifteen minutes—maybe
twenty—he would slip out of her bed and then out of her
life. She shouldn't want a little more time with him but she
did: just an hour, or a day or two, here in this magical town.

Remy brushed her hand through the light, crisp layer of
hair on Bo's chest. She rubbed her cheek against his shoulder before succumbing to the urge to bury her face in his
strong neck, silently asking him to stay exactly where he
was. She'd barely finished the thought when she felt the
tap of his fingers against her hip, and she pulled her head
back to look at him.

'I must go. I have to be up in a couple of hours.'

Remy sat up and managed a small smile as he swung
his legs around to sit on the edge of the bed. 'I'm leaving
early too.'

He reached behind him and squeezed her calf. 'I'm not
going to ask you where you're going because I might be
tempted to follow. I had a great time.'

Remy, holding the sheet up above her breasts, risked
placing her hand on his shoulder and turned her intended

caress into a quick pat. 'Me too. I thought we'd spontaneously combust that first time.'

His deep, sexy chuckle danced across her bare skin. 'We shouldn't have started kissing in the lift. We gave that other couple quite an eyeful.'

Remy frowned, confused. 'There was another couple in the lift?'

Bo stood up and pulled his boxers on. Placing his hands on his hips, he looked down at her, his mouth twisted into a wry smile. 'Yeah, there was.'

Remy tossed her head and didn't break contact with his mesmerising eyes. They were the most amazing shade of grey, edged with a ring of black. 'Well, sorry... I was kind of distracted.'

His eyes deepened and looked smoky again. 'I like the fact that I can make you lose track of your surroundings.'

Remy had to smile at the very self-satisfied smirk on his face.

When he'd headed to the bathroom Remy scuttled out of bed, rummaged in her suitcase and eventually found a pair of sleeping shorts and a roomy T-shirt. In the mirror on the opposite wall she saw her reflection and pulled a face at her very messy hair and make-up-free face. She wasn't looking her best, but what was the point of fussing over what she looked like when he was heading out through the door?

Out of her life.

One night. His staying any longer was not an option.

She shouldn't want him to stay at all.

Bo stood in the generic hotel bathroom and stared at his reflection in the large mirror above the basin. *This is a one-night stand,* he told himself, *a one-time deal.*

So what if it had been some of the best sex of his life? He'd spent two hours with her and they had done it...he could hardly believe it…*three* times. He wasn't in his dotage, but that was excessive even for him. He hadn't been able to stop touching her, seemingly desperate to make every second count.

He didn't want to walk back out there, pick his clothes up off the floor and walk out of her life. For the first time in far too many years he wasn't racing to leave, wasn't feeling the noose around his neck, the let-down after good sex with no emotional connection. All he wanted to do was to climb back into her bed and slide on home.

But that would not be sensible or practical and definitely not wise. Apart from the fact that she intrigued him—which he didn't like—they were out of condoms. Although if he didn't leave—*now!*—then he wasn't sure he'd be able to control himself.

Bo flipped on the cold tap and ducked his head under the spout, hoping the cold water would shock some sense into him. Why was he thinking about her like this? She was sex, pure and simple—a good time, and that was it!

She'd offered, he'd accepted, they'd both had fun—the *end*. He should be walking out through the door with a fat smile on his face.

She'd been a superb lay—the best two hours of his life…so why wasn't he feeling any better? Bo rubbed a towel over his hair and his hand over his jaw, now covered with dark stubble.

Since Ana he'd consciously, deliberately, kept all his sexual encounters casual and this had been supposed to be the most casual of all. A pretty girl—a tourist—someone he wouldn't see again. How much more casual could he get? He didn't know her surname, where she was from, what her cell number was, but she was the first woman in five years who'd managed to reach inside his gut and twist it into a knot.

And that was why he purposely, deliberately, strode

back into the room and quickly yanked on his clothes. The quicker he left, the quicker he could go back to thinking straight…

Remy had left the bed and got dressed and Bo was thankful for the small mercy that she wasn't still naked; that would have made leaving a lot harder than it already was. Than *he* already was…

He sent her a quick look. She sat on the corner of the bed, her long legs crossed at the knees. She looked cool and composed, so he walked over to her and dropped his head to kiss her high on her cheekbone, knowing that if he didn't keep it light he wouldn't be able to resist temptation…*again*.

'Thanks, Remy. Have a good life.'

'Yeah, you too.'

Bo yanked open the door, closed it behind him and shook his head. If someone had told him earlier that walking away from her would be difficult he would have told them that they had rocks in their head. Walking away was *never* difficult…

Except that this time it really was.

CHAPTER TWO

Six weeks later

IN PORTLAND, REMY stood in the smallest bedroom, which her mum had turned into a nursery for Callum, and kept her eyes firmly fixed on her baby half-brother's face. Only the fact that her mother would kill her if she woke Callum kept her from running into the dark Portland night, screaming like a psychotic banshee.

She was on the edge of sanity and there were more than a few contributing factors...

Six weeks in her mother's orbit was about five weeks and five days too long. As it turned out Callum slept a lot, and Jan had had plenty of time to nag her adult child.

'When are you going to pick up your career? You have an obligation to use the brains God gave you for something more worthwhile than catching flights, learning another way to cook fish and then blogging about it. All that education wasted. You are *not* fulfilling your potential.'

Below those comments were the unsaid implications... *You disappoint me. I expected more. What you* do *is important—not who* you *are.*

But she now had a bigger problem than her mother's nagging her about her life...

Remy looked down at the plastic wand in her hand and pulled another two out of her back pocket. One displayed a plus sign, one showed two lines and, just to make sure she got the message, the third had the word 'pregnant' in the display window.

She was going to have a baby.

This couldn't be happening...

She was going to have Bo's baby. The stranger from Bellevue. Her one-night, blow-her-head-off stand.

Remy slid down the wall and rested her head just below the butt of the happy giraffe painted on the wall. *God!* Why, oh, *why* was this happening to her? She *couldn't* be pregnant—she didn't *want* to be pregnant—but she held the irrefutable proof in her hands. And *how*? Bo had entered her only once, maybe twice, without a condom. On neither occasion had he been close to his happy ending... The man had had incredible self-control and he'd used that control to bring her to orgasm after orgasm during the night.

But apparently one of his super-sperm had sneaked out and had been hell-bent on finding its own happy ending. With *her* egg.

Remy muttered a series of silent curse words as tears pooled in her eyes.

In his wooden crib Callum snuffled and Remy tensed, thinking that he was about to wake up. She stretched her neck to look at him. Crap! She was going to have one of... of *those*! They didn't even look all that interesting to have around; all Callum seemed to do was cry, eat and sleep.

She wanted to send hers back... Why didn't life come with a remote control? *Whoops, didn't mean to do that— rewind. Don't like that channel—swap.*

Remy banged her head lightly against the wall. *Life doesn't work that way, chicken.* She couldn't duck, ignore or rewrite her life or her past...no matter how much she'd like to.

Remy stared at the carpet between her knees. She was

her mother's daughter in more ways than one: stupid when it came to condom use, apparently, but brilliant academically.

Like her brainy mother—a professor in mechanical engineering—she'd been in an accelerated learning programme most of her life and at sixteen had started at the same Ivy League college Jan was a lecturer at. She'd spent her entire undergraduate degree years feeling that she was an exhibit, her mum's pet project…paraded around when she was in favour, held at a distance when she wasn't.

After completing her PhD in computer science she'd been headhunted by Tiscot's, the biggest media and PR company in the country, to be their Chief Information Officer at a stupidly massive salary. Her desire to please and to achieve had followed her into the workplace, and she'd given the company, and her boss, more than a pound of her flesh—part of her soul as well.

Her life had been consumed by work, and such dedication, obsession, such *stupidity*, had caused her ulcer to perforate and she'd landed up in hospital—which had given her some much needed time to think.

Lying in that hospital bed, she'd never felt more alone. She'd had no visitors—why would she? She had no friends—and the only flowers she'd received had been from the firm, probably ordered by the junior receptionist. Long, long hours on her own had given her the time to examine her life and she had come to accept that she was twenty-five, lonely—because she never made an effort to make friends—perpetually single—because she never took the time to date—and desperately unhealthy because she never took the time to eat properly.

She was also burnt out and possibly depressed. And every time she thought about returning to Tiscot's the flames of hell fired up in her stomach.

That had been a freaking big clue that she'd had a choice

to make: she had to change her life or allow hell to move permanently into her stomach. She'd chosen to save herself and her sanity and had walked away from her corporate, high-pressure, immensely demanding job.

From New York she'd flown to England, but that hadn't quite been far enough to silence her mother's voice in her head constantly reminding her that she was making a huge mistake, that she was being a coward, a cop-out. That she wasn't good enough, wasn't working hard enough, wasn't achieving enough.

The rest of Europe had still been too close, so she'd headed for Asia, and by the time she'd got to Africa Jan's voice had been quieter. But sadly it still hadn't disappeared entirely.

Leaving her corporate life had been the right decision, Remy thought. And she'd seen some amazing places, met some extraordinary people. But travelling hadn't filled all the holes in her soul. She was still looking for…

Remy racked her brain. Why couldn't she define what she was seeking? Why did she have this belief that she would only know what it was when she found it? It wasn't love, or a man, or a relationship—love was conditional, an iffy emotion that wasn't steadfast and true. And, as she'd been shown all her life, it could be used as a weapon or a bribe. She had spent her life chasing it, catching it and then having it ripped from her grasp. She was *so* over it.

As a result, she didn't buy in to the premise that love, or a man, would make her happy. So what *would*? She wished she knew.

Was she looking for a new job? Possibly. A new passion? Definitely.

What she *hadn't* been looking for was pregnancy or incipient motherhood. That was taking her whole turn-over-a-new-leaf attitude a forest too far.

But a baby was on its way, she was keeping it, and

she had to adjust. She had to make plans—start thinking for two.

But before she could make plans she had to tell Bo—tell him that she was pregnant and expecting his child. Bo deserved to know he'd fathered a child, and her child needed to know who his or her father was. She knew this because nearly thirty years ago, in a rare display of loss of control, her mum had gone to a party, got totally high, and couldn't remember exactly who she'd slept with that night.

As a result Remy didn't have a cookin' clue *who* her own father was.

Telling Bo was the *one* thing she was sure of. She owed him that. She supposed that she would also have to tell her family…which meant—unfortunately—having a conversation with her mother.

Remy sighed and pushed her hair back off her face as she stood up. That was going to be fun. Jan would respond as if she'd told her that she was intending to juggle with vials of something lethal. It was going to be ten times worse than telling her mother that she had given up her job to go travelling to 'find' herself.

Way. Way. Worse.

Unlike travelling, she couldn't just give up a baby and resume the life Jan had spent so much time planning.

Remy walked over to the crib and stared down at the tiny, tiny little bundle who was her mother's latest little project. *Unfair,* Remy thought, biting her lip. Her mum loved Callum and she loved her. Sort of…

'I'll try to shield you as much as I can, little brother, but I'm warning you she's a force of nature. Don't be too smart, okay?' she murmured, touching the back of her knuckle to his satin-smooth head. 'I'm going to leave Portland now—tonight. I've got to get out of here. And, no, I'm not quite brave enough to tell her yet.'

'Tell her what?' Jan asked from the doorway, her arms folded against her already flat stomach.

Her body wouldn't *dare* rebel and hold on to its baby fat a minute longer than it should, Remy thought.

Remy pushed the pregnancy test wands back into her pocket, hiding them, before turning to face her mum. 'Nothing much,' she lied. 'Just that I'm leaving. It's time.'

Jan nodded briskly. 'Good. I was about to suggest the same thing. But before you go I want to tell you about a VP position that I hear is vacant at Repcal Tech. It's a step down from where you were before, but beggars can't be choosers…'

Back in Bellevue, Remy thought as she pulled into a spare parking space in front of the diner on the corner of Main and First. Looking down, she saw the open notebook next to her on the cracked bench seat of her old Ford 150. There were just two bullet points on the blank page.

Fill up with gas.
Find Bo and tell him you're pregnant.

Easy-peasy, lemon-squeezy, she assured herself. Once she told Bo that he was going to be a daddy and that she expected absolutely nothing from him she could move on again. He would be upset at the news—and then grateful when he heard that she intended to let him off the hook, happy that she didn't need or expect anything from him. Then she'd leave…

She had, she reckoned, another three months of travelling before she had to make some hard decisions—like where she wanted to live, what she was going to do for the rest of her life.

That's what happens when you let yourself play with fire, Draycott. You get burned, dummy.

Or, in her case, pregnant…

Remy grabbed her leather tote bag and left the car, slamming the heavy door shut behind her. She had been travelling for hours and she was hungry and desperate to use the bathroom.

Remy pushed open the door to the diner and sighed when she saw the packed tables and booths. Apparently lunchtime on a Saturday was chaotic. She used the facilities and washed her hands and face, taking some time to run a brush through her hair, to swipe on some lip gloss. This was Bo's town, after all, and she didn't want to run into him looking as if she'd been dragged backwards through a bush.

And if she *did* run into him, how should she tell him?

Hi, remember me? Thought you'd like to know that I'm pregnant.

Funny thing… You know when you slipped inside without a condom? Well, it had a pretty big consequence…

Or her favourite.

I'm pregnant. It's yours. Bye.

Remy sighed at her pale reflection in the bathroom mirror before whirling away and heading back into the diner. Food always made her feel better. She'd have a bacon and blue cheese burger and then she'd tackle the problem of finding out exactly who Bo actually was and how to get hold of him. Once she did that her duty would be done and she could move on.

There still wasn't an empty table in the place, so Remy looked over the customers to see who would be most receptive to sharing a table. Years of travelling had robbed her of any lingering shyness and she could talk to anybody, anywhere. There were two good-looking blondes, one male, one female, sitting in a corner booth. They looked enough alike for her to assume that they were siblings. And, since they weren't lovers, they shouldn't mind her horning in on their private time.

Her mind made up, Remy walked across the room to the booth and flashed them her biggest smile. Ooh, the blond guy was *very* fine: muscled and masculine, with a gorgeous pair of deep brown eyes.

Rein it in, Draycott. The last time you flirted with a hot man you ended up with a lot more than you bargained for.

So Remy dialled down her smile and gestured to the empty seats. 'I'm absolutely starving and I was wondering if I could share your table. Please?'

The elfin face of the woman was tilted up and she smiled back. 'Sure…' She scooted up on the bench and patted the empty space next to her. 'Take a seat. I'm Ginny, and this is my cousin Eli.'

Eli leaned back and gave her a long, lazy smile.

Yeah, definitely flirting material… Except that he didn't do anything for her. The eyes were brown, not grey, his hair was too light and his smile was too open.

'I'm Remy.'

'Are you passing through?' Eli asked.

'I might be around for a couple of days—a week, maybe.'

It didn't seem that big a town—surely it wouldn't take that long to track Bo down? Maybe she could ask Eli and Ginny if they knew him. But later, after they'd all eaten.

She gestured to their half-eaten plates of food—salad for her, burger for him—and to their cooling coffee. 'Don't let me interrupt your conversation, please.'

Remy quietly ordered her food from a waitress as the cousins resumed their discussion around organic farming. Remy, not knowing anything about farming, and even less about organic farming, tuned out and leaned back and closed her eyes. Lord, she was tired. Soul-deep tired… Thank goodness she'd booked a room at the hotel down the street before she'd left Portland. After her burger she'd check in and maybe just lie down for a little while.

'Did you see the sample menus from the chef candidates that were faxed through from LA?' Ginny was asking.

'Yeah…not that I read them,' Eli answered.

She'd said the magic word 'menus' and Remy couldn't help tuning in.

'I bet you he didn't explain the brief properly—the vision of the restaurant,' Ginny grumbled. 'They're too far out. We don't want Turkish eggs and caviar omelettes…'

'What are Turkish eggs?' Eli demanded.

'Poached eggs, basically,' Remy murmured, unable to help herself. 'Although I do mine with mint, chilli and smoked paprika. Seriously yummy.'

'Maybe we *do* want Turkish eggs on the menu,' Eli told Ginny.

'Well, I don't want caviar omelettes. Caviar omelettes do *not* belong in the type of place we are opening at Belleaire,' Ginny said obstinately.

Belleaire… Remy thought. The fancy wine estate on the outskirts of town. Were Eli and Ginny two of the three family members who owned and ran the upmarket, famous estate which was prominently featured in all the tourist brochures?

Okay, she wasn't going to pretend that she wasn't listening any more. 'What type of restaurant are you opening?' she asked, intrigued.

Ginny pushed her coffee cup away and half turned to face Remy. 'A family place—breakfasts, teas, light lunches. Fresh, healthy, light, interesting food that's not… *pretentious*. I want people to be able to relax, to bring their kids there, but still be able to get a nice meal, a decent glass of wine.' She pulled out a sheaf of papers from her bag and slapped them onto the table. 'My brother is currently interviewing candidates for the manager-cum-chef position and he's asked them to send through sample menus for what they would do if they were offered the position.'

Remy gestured to the papers. 'Can I look?'

'Are you a chef?'

Remy shook her head. 'No, but I *am* a cook and I adore food. I've done about a million cookery courses.' She skimmed through the menus, tossed most of them aside and kept a couple in another pile. She tapped her finger against the slim pile. 'These here are the best of a bad bunch, but they're still not great.'

Eli folded his arms and his biceps bulged. Nice arms, wide chest, flat stomach... But still she felt nothing. Weird.

'What would *you* do?'

She blinked at him. 'About what?'

'If it was your place? You obviously know food, and you seem to be familiar with the dishes on those menus.'

'Oh...' Remy thought for a minute, her face cupped in her hands. 'Um...interesting salads. Couscous and butternut, watermelon and feta—things like that. Soups with crusty, gorgeous bread. Hearty dishes like lamb stew, lasagne and chicken casserole. Classic puddings with one or two exceptions to keep things interesting. A specially designed menu for kids—but I'd avoid burgers and hot dogs. Fish and chips, a chicken pasta dish—meals that kids like and mums like them eating.'

Remy didn't notice the long look Ginny and Eli exchanged. Instead her eyes were on the waitress, who was walking in their direction with what was, hopefully, her burger. She was so hungry she could eat a horse.

'Are you looking for work?' Ginny asked.

'Sorry? What?' Remy sighed her disappointment when her burger went to the table two up from them.

'We're looking for a chef-manager to set up the bistro and you seem to know what you're talking about,' Ginny explained, her face animated with excitement.

'Uh… I wasn't planning on sticking around,' Remy replied, her mind whirling.

She was here to talk to Bo and then she was on her way. But setting up a restaurant, designing a menu, building something from the ground up, sounded like a whole bunch of fun.

Throughout her life, and despite trying many different activities on her travels, food had seemed to be her only constant. When she was a child, battling to reconcile her intellect with her emotions, Grandma Rosie had often hauled out her baking bowl and flour and put her to work. Baking calmed her and it and cooking was still her favourite means of stress relief.

When she'd started travelling she had finally had the time to indulge her passion; she'd started to blog about food and spent an enormous amount of time seeking out the best food markets, learning how to cook the local foods.

She'd taken a course in how to cook Thai food in Bangkok, had done a confectionery course in London, a *cordon bleu* course in Marseille. Sushi in Sydney. Chinese in… Sydney again. She seemed to gravitate towards the food industry, but she didn't want the pressure of working in a professional kitchen.

If she weren't pregnant she wouldn't hesitate to take Ginny up on her offer. But after seeing Bo she needed to keep moving while she still could. Some time in the next four months she had to find a town or a city she wanted to live in and—*ack!*—a job. Or, better, a business that covered her daily expenses and allowed her flexibility and freedom.

A cupcake shop? An ice cream parlour? An old-fashioned tea room?

And where? In Portland? Close to her mum and to Grandmother Rosie, who'd helped raise her?

'Do you have another job? Somewhere to be?' Ginny

demanded, breaking into Remy's thoughts. She pointed a finger at her. 'I can see that you are intrigued and interested, and life is too short to spend your time doing stuff you don't like.'

She knew that—that was why she didn't have an ulcer any more. A baby, but not an ulcer.

'I *am* interested...it *does* sound like fun.' Remy tipped her head, thinking quickly. 'Maybe I could spend a week or so here, look over the space and draw up some sample menus. I could possibly cook a couple of dishes that you can sample. I can't commit to a taking a job right now—to *anything* right now—but I'd be happy to give you guys some ideas, so that when you do employ someone you can tell them what you want and not have to rely on their taste.'

Ginny clapped her hands in delight. '*Would* you? That sounds amazing. Of course we'd pay you for your time.'

'Hell, I'd pay you to cook for me,' Eli stated. 'So, how long have you been travelling for?'

'Ages.' Remy smiled at him and his returning smile showed interest. She checked inside herself again... No flutter, no tingle—nothing. *Damn.*

Eli must have seen something cross her face, because his eyes laughed at her before he softly spoke again. 'Huh, I must be losing my touch. That doesn't happen often.'

He said it with such genuine regret and confusion that she couldn't hold his arrogant statement against him. So she shrugged and smiled, genuinely regretful. 'Sorry.'

'I've lost track of this conversation,' Ginny muttered.

'I've lost track of my burger,' Remy stated, desperate to change the subject. 'Oh, good—it's on its way.'

The waitress slipped her plate in front of her with a murmured apology about the delay. Remy waved her away—and then blanched as the smell of fried onions hit her nose. Swallowing down her sudden nausea, which she attributed to her being on the *very* wrong side of ravenous, she cut into her burger and pulled it apart. She'd ordered it rare, as she always did, and the patty was perfectly cooked, oozing juice.

Her stomach climbed up into her throat and Remy slapped her hand over her mouth.

Ginny frowned. 'Hey, are you okay?'

Remy shook her head and pushed her plate away. She had to get out of here. *Now!*

Scrabbling for her bag, she stood up, teetering on her feet. Eli flew up and grabbed her arm, keeping her from doing a face-plant on the floor.

'I think I'm going to be sick,' she muttered to no one in particular.

From a long way away she heard Eli speaking to Ginny. 'Maybe you should take her to wherever she's staying, Gin, and I'll settle the bill.'

Before she knew it the pint-sized Ginny had a surprisingly strong arm around her waist and was guiding her out of the restaurant.

So…okay, then, she thought as she sucked in fresh air. Maybe she *wasn't* going to be one of those lucky women who got to skate through pregnancy.

Bo looked at his watch. He had ten minutes before his meeting with Ginny and Eli, and he was thinking, as he always did, that he was lucky to have his sister and his cousin as full partners in the family business. They fought like cats and dogs, but implicitly trusted each other, and each of them had their strengths, their place in the business.

His was the business brain and he kept the whole ship sailing smoothly, Eli made the exceptional wines the business was built on, and Ginny was the farmer, the viticulturist: responsible for looking after the vines and the land, the olive orchard and the vegetable gardens that supplied the mansion hotel and the restaurants with fresh produce.

On paper and in the eyes of their staff he was the boss, but in reality they operated as a rough sort of democracy. Any major decisions were made collectively, through negotiation and compromise. Sometimes that negotiation and compromise sounded more like shouting and arguing, but whatever worked...

And it *did* work. Better than any of them would have believed when they'd inherited equal shares of the winery, house and land after their beloved grandfather had passed on ten years before. He and Ginny had supported Eli when he'd informed them that he needed to travel, to visit other wine-producing countries, and he and Eli had trusted Ginny's instincts to restore the Belleaire mansion to its former glory when they'd decided to turn it into a hotel. They'd both stood at his side when he'd buried his wife of six months...

Ana.

So little time as man and wife and he ached remembering that their marriage hadn't been the happiest time of their relationship. As always, before he forced those thoughts away he consoled himself with the reminder that he'd known her and loved her one way or another all his life. She'd been his childhood friend, his first girlfriend, his prom date. They'd broken up during college but had reconnected in their mid-twenties when she'd become his live-in lover, his fiancée, and finally, for far too short a time, his wife.

And, to date, the only woman he'd ever loved. Would ever love.

Ignoring the issue that cropped up after they married, he deliberately remembered that they had suited each other perfectly. He was ambitious and dynamic and driven, able to take control and to be in charge. He had grounded her. She'd been sanguine and scatty, easy-going and happy to let him do what he did best—which had been to make the decisions and to chart the course of their lives. They'd been the perfect example of opposites attracting, and lightning, Bo thought, shoving his hands into his pockets as he stared out of his office window at the sun setting over the western vineyard, didn't strike twice. He'd had the real thing. The *only* thing…

They said that memories of the people you'd lost faded, but even after four and a half years Bo didn't need to look at the large black-and-white photograph that dominated the credenza next to his desk to visualise Ana. The long blonde hair he'd used to love wrapping around his fists as he slid into her, her dirty laugh, her wide blue eyes. Sometimes he swore he could still smell her…

She was still as much a part of him as she had been… she always would be. Love didn't die with death. Or because of a rolling, on-off six month argument.

'I'll love you to the end…' he'd told her as the light of life had faded from her eyes, as she'd lain in his arms, battered and broken, in that driving rain. She'd needed to hear it and he'd needed to say it.

She'd managed a final tiny smile. 'Promise?'

'Yeah. Always.'

He glanced at the photograph and his heart contracted. He was still in love with his wife—would always be in love with his wife. Despite everything that had happened, he'd never stopped loving her. As a result he liked women but he didn't engage with them emotionally…financially. When you'd had something so amazing nobody else could compete—and he wasn't prepared for them to try.

And if the fact that he was still in love with his wife wasn't enough to put him off getting involved with a woman, then his job was. His career demanded eighty-hour weeks or more—when would he have time to date, for a relationship?

Nah, he was happy to play it cool, skimming along the surface…

Then his thoughts veered off on a tangent, as they often did lately, and the image of Remy—naked, looking down at him, her pale eyes warm with laughter—appeared behind his retina. Remy, his hot-as-hell, over-before-daylight, one-night lover. He could remember every kiss, every touch, every smell and he wished he could forget. One of these days he'd stop thinking of her…of that mind-blowing night.

Hopefully it would be sometime soon, so that his life could go back to normal. He hadn't seen another woman, hadn't had sex for six weeks, and it was time—way past time—to replace those hot memories of the champagne-eyed witch with the very bad pickup lines.

A hand slapping his desk jerked him back to the present. Eli and Ginny were on the other side of his desk, looking at him expectantly. When had they come in? He hadn't even noticed.

'Hi…what's up?'

Ginny and Eli exchanged a long, weird look. 'You called us to a meeting, Bo,' Ginny said, pushing her hair behind her ears. 'Are you okay?'

That would be a negative.

'Sure,' he lied, hating the feeling of operating on only one or two cylinders. He ran a multimillion-dollar company—it was time he acted like the super-sharp business-man he was reputed to be. Remembering his wife was normal—to be expected, even—but daydreaming about a hot night with a woman he wouldn't see again was not. It was utterly ridiculous…

Irritated with himself, he located the file he needed from a pile to his right and tossed it across the table to where his sister and cousin were now sitting.

Dropping into his leather chair, he leaned back and placed his feet on the corner of his desk. 'Bella's Folly.'

Ginny leaned forward, clasping her hands around her knees. 'The land with no owner?'

'That we know of. If there isn't a will, then the estate will pass on to her nearest relative. If there is a will, then it's simple. Either way, we need to find the heir first,' Eli said, placing his ankle on his knee.

'Yeah. There is going to be a *lot* of interest in the property.' Bo leaned further back in his chair. 'Moving on from one folly to another… The renovations for the bistro and coffee shop are nearly finished, and I'm flying to New York tonight and will be back tomorrow evening. I need to see some customers, talk to some distributors, and I'll also interview a couple of chefs for the position of the bistro chef/manager while I'm out there.'

Eli frowned. 'No candidates from California?'

'A couple,' Bo answered. 'These are better qualified.'

'We met someone today who had real potential. Someone who knew food and whom we really liked,' Ginny mused. 'She could be just what we're looking for.'

Bo lifted his eyebrows. 'Is she applying for the job?'

Ginny pulled a face. 'She's not sticking around that long—which is a pity, because I think she would've been perfect for the bistro.'

Comme ci, comme ça… Bo shrugged. 'I'll find someone in New York.'

Ginny shook her head. 'Just remember that we need the right *personality*. Someone who will fit in here at Belleaire with us. We want someone who is warm and funny, who can talk to kids and adults alike. Someone who has brilliant people skills and a solid sense of humour,' Ginny insisted.

The last person *he'd* come across with a solid sense of humour had turned out to be the best sex of his life.

Better than Ana? Really?

Different from Ana, he quickly amended. Very different. *I thought we were done thinking about her, moron?*

'It would be nice if she was a looker, too.' Eli added.

Remy had been a looker...

Enough, Tessier!

Bo looked at his watch. 'I need to get going. Don't do anything stupid while I'm away, okay?'

Eli sent Ginny a sardonic look. 'How old are we? Ten?'

'One of these days he'll realise that he isn't actually the boss of us,' Ginny replied.

'Somebody needs to keep you two in line,' Bo told them, and held up his hand as mouths opened to protest. 'Yeah, I know. I'm arrogant, annoying and bossy.' He smiled at the two people he loved best. 'Now, get out of my office. I've got a lot to do before I head to the airport.'

Eli and Ginny, not in the least offended, stood up. Ginny, being Ginny, walked around his desk to give him a hug goodbye. It didn't matter if he was going away for two days or two years. Ginny would hug him as if he was leaving for ever.

CHAPTER THREE

THE BELLEAIRE WINE estate was dominated by a triple storey blue stone mansion—and how could it not be? Remy thought, pulling to the side of the broad, Spanish-oak-tree-lined driveway so that she could spend a minute admiring the house.

It had turrets and bay windows galore, balconies and buttresses, and was three storeys of pure whimsy. It looked like a grand old lady who'd had too many glasses of wine at suppertime and had decided to kick up her heels and dance a jig. It was loud and ostentatious and a tad over the top—and she absolutely loved it.

Her type of mansion, Remy thought.

The entrance to the hotel was just behind a massive square fountain, and there were discreet signs directing visitors to the art gallery, the craft shop, the potters' studio. In the other direction was the tasting room, and if she looked to the land there were rows of vines as far as the eye could see, heavy with grapes. It was late summer and autumn was on its way. Some of the trees were starting to turn and she knew that the harvest was fast approaching.

Remy, as directed by Ginny, took the path to the gallery and walked through the luscious gardens to her destination. God, it was pretty. How lucky were Ginny and Eli to own this, to be part of this? Remy looked around. The place was elegant, rich, tasteful…and Remy was *still* surprised that Ginny had invited her to see Belleaire up close and to join her and Eli for supper that night.

Remy felt heat in her cheekbones, still felt humiliated and foolish. After her mortifying display in the diner she'd shrugged off Ginny's company in the hotel reception area and stumbled up to her room, deathly tired and intensely humiliated, and had instantly dropped to her knees in front of the toilet.

She hadn't really left that bathroom since. God knew how she was going to manage eating with Eli and Ginny… She was still living on crackers, apples and cheese—none of which she could keep down. Dinner would be a nightmare. Right now, her best plan would be to tell them she was pregnant and that she'd just have a soft drink with them—she couldn't even drink wine on a wine estate, for Pete's sake!—and leave early.

Passing the art gallery, she saw another building with a sign stating that it was the Blue View Bistro and she grinned. Belleaire, Bellevue, Blue View…that worked, she thought. She pulled open the door and stepped into the large, mostly empty space.

On the wall closest to her was an artist's impression of what the restaurant would look like and Remy approved of the bright colours, fun artwork and welcoming vibe. There would be vintage mismatched chairs and tables, modern light fittings, and couches and chairs grouped in amongst the tables. It would be a fantastic mix of old and new… *Damn*, she wished that she'd be able to see it when it was done.

'Remy, you made it!'

Remy looked towards the bright voice and saw Ginny coming out from an area that was to be the bar. Surprising her, Ginny kissed both her cheeks before looking up into her face.

'How are you feeling? Better? I hope so. Come into

the bar area. My cousin and brother are having an argument about bar stools. You're still looking very pale and washed out.'

Great. Good to know. 'Um…'

'What was it? Stomach flu?' Ginny guided her over to the door to the bar and yanked it open.

Well, here goes, Remy thought, stepping into a room dominated by a massive bar. She'd consider it a practice round for when she told her child's sexy father. And, dear Lord, he'd been *so* sexy…

Focus, Remy.

'Uh, no. I'm pregnant, and that was my very first bout of morning sickness—henceforth to be known as all-day sickness.' She kept her eyes firmly on Ginny's face. 'Actually, I came to tell you that I can't do supper. I can't keep much down. The reason I'm in Bellevue is to tell the father that I'm pregnant with his baby.'

'Remy?'

It was the voice from her dreams—the one she still heard in her ear, against her skin. The one she heard in the memories she relived over and over again every night. That deep rumble, capable of sending heat to her womb, prickling her skin.

'Bo?'

He was dressed in battered jeans and an open-necked white shirt, sleeves rolled up to reveal raised veins on those tanned forearms. He was here—all six-foot-something of pure, pissed off male.

He got up slowly and she saw that his eyes were slate-grey and hard.

'What did you just say?'

What *had* she just said? She was so flabbergasted by his presence that she couldn't remember… Oh, hell. Pregnant. His baby.

Oh, heavens, why did these things keep happening to her?

Remy bit her bottom lip and folded her arms across her chest, thinking about damage control. 'Um…obviously I didn't mean to tell you like that…'

'You're *pregnant*?' Bo shouted, and she winced as his words bounced off the walls.

'Yes.'

Was it hot in here? she wondered as the floor rose and fell. Along with heat there was suddenly no air. Instinctively she reached out her hand and grabbed the edge of the bar to keep from falling over. She saw dots behind her eyes, felt the blackness coming closer.

The last thing she heard before crumpling to the floor was Eli's amused comment. 'Well, now, isn't *this* interesting?'

When she came to she was on the floor, her back against a solid male chest and two strong arms criss-crossed over her chest. She sat within the V of two legs, long thighs pressing against her own. She felt warm and secure and so very, *very* tired. Ginny was on her haunches in front of her and had a damp linen napkin in her hand, which she lifted to run across her forehead.

'Hey, you're back,' Ginny said quietly, her expression concerned.

'What happened?' Remy asked weakly.

Eli dropped to her level, rested his arm on his bent knee and handed her a quirky smile. 'Well, sunshine, you kind of announced that you were pregnant with Bo's baby and then you dropped like a stone.'

'When did you last eat? Are you getting enough rest? Vitamins?' Ginny demanded.

Remy pushed her hair out of her eyes. 'Bo…?'

She felt those strong arms tense before she heard his voice in her ear. 'Still here.'

Thank God. No, that wasn't right… She shouldn't *like* being in his arms. Shouldn't feel as if she was finally where she was meant to be…

Get a grip, Draycott!

He wasn't her man…this wasn't her place…

'Are you still feeling like you're going to faint?' he demanded, moving his hands to hold her hips.

She winced at the irritation in his voice. Well, it wasn't as if she'd done it on purpose. She touched her forehead and shook her head. 'No. I think I'm fine.'

His fingers dug into her skin. 'Be sure. I don't want to have to catch you again.'

Remy angled her head so that she could look at him. His mouth was drawn into a thin line and his jaw was rock-hard with tension. 'You caught me?'

'The man can move when he has incentive to do so,' Eli said in an amused drawl.

'Shut up, Elijah,' Bo snapped, and he scooted backwards and stood up.

Reaching for Remy's hands, he pulled her up into a standing position and kept a hand on her elbow—she supposed, to keep her from falling. Which was at odds with the furious expression on his face, which suggested that he'd like to boot her off the nearest cliff.

Could she blame him? Remy sighed. Not really. She had delivered her tilt-his-world-upside-down news with absolutely no finesse and then fallen to the floor.

Then again, his wasn't the only world that had been affected. He, at least, got to walk away. She didn't have the luxury of that choice. So Remy straightened her shoulders, lifted her chin and looked him dead in the eye. 'I'm pregnant. You're the father. That's all I wanted to say.'

Remy saw her bag on the table, so walked over to it

and pulled it over her shoulder. She dredged up a smile for Eli and Ginny.

'Sorry I spoilt your evening, and for fainting…for dropping this bombshell like I did. I seem to make a habit of looking like an idiot around you. So…I'm going to go now.'

Not waiting for their response, she turned and walked to the door leading to the restaurant, fighting back tears. *Why?* It wasn't as if she'd expected anything from him, and she didn't need anything from him. She wove her way between the tables and finally reached the front door. Pulling it open, she stepped outside and sucked in deep breaths of warm, early-evening air.

Placing her hand on her still flat stomach, she gave it a quick pat. 'Well, it's you and me, babe. And we'll be fine.'

Remy turned as the door behind her was wrenched open and Bo stalked out.

'Remy!'

Remy tipped her head as Bo walked down the path towards her. Oh, dear… The branch was back up his butt: he was now cool, calm and thoroughly in control. Unreadable eyes and a 'let's fix this' expression on his face. He stopped a foot away from her and she was reminded that this was a powerful man in his prime.

'We need to talk,' he stated.

'I think we've covered the high points,' Remy said.

'We haven't even started,' Bo replied, his voice low but determined. He placed his hand under her elbow. 'Let's go.'

Remy wrenched her arm out of his grip. 'I don't think so!'

Bo looked upwards, as if he were searching for patience. 'We need to talk and we are *going* to talk. You don't get to drop into my life again, tell me that you're pregnant and that I'm responsible, and then just walk out again. That's not how it works!'

Remy twisted her lips and looked down at her toes.

Of course they had to talk—she knew that—but just not right now. Not when she was feeling weak and foolish and so very, *very* tired. She just wanted some distance from him—to regroup, to stop thinking about how gorgeous he looked in those casual clothes, how much she wished she were in his arms, touching him, being loved by him.

These pregnancy hormones were playing havoc with her emotions. She just needed some time, some space… She needed to *think*.

Lifting a hand, she looked at the vineyards beyond his shoulder and forced words out. 'We'll talk…but not now. I have a cracking headache and I am really tired. Maybe tomorrow?'

Bo just looked at her for a long, long time before nodding. 'You do look like hell—and like a puff of wind could blow you over.'

Remy sighed her relief. 'Okay, then. I'll see you—' She squawked in dismay when Bo slid her bag off her shoulder and immediately slid the zip open. Like a typical man, he shoved his hand inside and rooted around. 'Hey! Give me my bag! What do you think you're doing?'

He pulled out her truck keys and dangled them in front of her nose before shoving them into the front pocket of his jeans. Remy just stared at him, not believing that he could pull such a Neanderthal stunt.

'You… What…? *Arrgh!* Why?'

Bo sent her a cold smile. 'I'm confiscating your keys because I have a sneaking suspicion that you might drive away and keep on going. And if you did I wouldn't know where to start looking for you. Talking of which…' He pulled her purse out of her bag and turned his back to her when she lunged for it. He quickly found her driver's licence and his height kept it out of her reach. 'Horrible photo of you… Remy Draycott, twenty-seven, formerly of the Upper West Side, Manhattan. Fancy…'

'Put it back.' Remy felt the enamel flying off her teeth as she ground them together. She watched as Bo replaced her driver's licence and closed her wallet, dropping it back into her bag. She tapped her foot and sent him a belligerent look. 'Are you done?'

'For now.' Bo wrapped the strap of her tote around his fist in that uniquely male way of carrying a woman's bag. He gestured to the path, silently suggesting that she start walking. 'We're going back to my place and we're going to talk. I'll bring you back to your truck later.'

'Give me back my keys and my bag and I will meet you tomorrow—at whatever time suits you.'

'*Now* suits me—and I don't trust you not to run,' Bo told her, his expression uncompromising. 'Frankly, I don't trust you at all.'

Remy watched, every sense on high alert, as Bo walked from the kitchen back to the lounge, a tumbler of whiskey in his hand and a cup of chamomile tea in the other. He placed her cup on the side table next to her and then, instead of sitting down on one of the long, plump leather couches that sat at right angles to the chair she was curled up in, he sat directly in front of her, on the handcrafted wooden table, and rested his forearms on his thighs.

She liked his open-plan wood and steel house, she thought. It was light and airy and he had good furniture. It needed a bit more colour, some art, some character, but it had a nice foundation.

Pity its owner was a pill.

She was still mightily unimpressed with him and his 'I'm confiscating your keys' and 'We're going to talk' statements.

Grunt. Grunt.

He was exactly the type of arrogant, domineering jerk she kept her distance from under normal circumstances.

Brusque, bolshie, bossy. She'd been raised in a feminist household by discussion and debate—with her mother always eventually getting her way—and it had been three years and a million miles since anyone—let alone a man—had presumed to tell her what to do.

She wasn't used to it and she didn't like it—and it didn't matter that he was unfairly gorgeous! All *that* meant was that he was perfect to frolic with.

But to deal with? To be the father of her baby?

Not so much…

Note to self: *Bad, bad—terrible—idea to fall pregnant by a man you do not know. Not good at all.*

Remy rubbed her hand across her forehead as she kicked off her sandals and tucked her feet under her bottom, turning so her cheek could rest on the back of the leather chair. She was comprehensively and utterly exhausted. She supposed she'd better get used to it, she thought. It was only going to get a lot worse.

Bo placed his glass on the coffee table and took her hand, holding it firmly in his when she tried to tug it away.

'What are you doing?' she squawked as lightning danced across her skin.

Bo placed the pad of his thumb into the valley between her hand and her thumb and squeezed. Remy nearly spilled her tea as pain radiated from the joint into her hand and up her arm.

'Stop! Jeez, that *hurts*!'

'Stop being such a baby,' Bo told her, keeping the pressure constant. 'I'm going to hold it for another thirty seconds, with a ten-second rest before we go again.'

Remy tugged, found she still couldn't dislodge his hand, and glared at him. 'And the point of this would be…?'

'Your headache. This is a pressure point. Your headache will go in a minute or two.'

'Rubbish!' Remy scoffed as he released the pressure.

But the weird thing was that her head *did* feel…well, lighter. It was still pounding, but not quite so badly.

Auto-suggestion, she told herself. It had nothing to do with those strong masculine fingers holding her hand.

'Ow! *Dammit!*' she howled when he resumed his torture. Although she had to admit that it was a sweet sort of pain…a healing pain. 'How did *you*, Mr Stick-Up-His-Ass, learn *this*?' she demanded.

'My wife was an acupuncturist and very into alternative medicine. I picked up a couple of tricks along the way,' Bo answered.

His eyes flickered with an emotion she couldn't identify. Sadness? Guilt?

He'd said that he was single and she believed him. So what had happened? There was only one way to find out.

'What happened to her? Did you get divorced?'

'Widowed. She died five years ago.'

Remy sucked her bottom lip between her teeth. 'I'm sorry…' she murmured.

'How's your head?' Bo asked, not bothering to be subtle about his desire to change the subject.

Remy frowned when she realised that her headache was practically gone. 'Huh? I can hardly feel it.'

'Good.'

'Thanks,' Remy said, tugging her hand out of his grasp. 'So—you wanted to talk?'

Bo, not saying anything, just stared at her for a long while and she struggled not to squirm. Those eyes should be considered a weapon of war, she decided. They could slice and dice with precision and icy control.

'We used condoms—how do you think this happened?'

She heard the disbelief in his voice and tried not to feel insulted. 'You don't remember that on round number two you slid on home *before* you put a condom on? You did the same thing on round three.'

She had a brief moment of pleasure when his eyes widened. He was obviously recalling that they *had* had unprotected sex. *Brief* unprotected sex, but enough to cause havoc in their lives.

Bo rubbed a hand over his jaw before waving at the air in the general direction of her stomach. 'And that was enough to…?'

'Obviously,' Remy replied. 'Look, Bo—I get that there are a million questions running through your head, but let's cut to the chase. You're the only guy I've slept with in more than two years. So, yeah, we can do the dog and pony show, argue about whether the kid is yours or not, but a paternity test will prove it is.'

She sighed.

'I know that you only signed up for a night of uncomplicated sex, not to be Daddy of the Year, so you don't need to worry about this… I'm perfectly happy to take this on single-handed.'

'Excuse me?'

Remy narrowed her eyes at his whippy voice. She tried again. 'You don't need to feel obligated.'

'We're discussing my child—not a freaking dinner engagement!' Bo said on a low growl.

Remy wasn't a fool. She saw that this was a man on the edge and thought that silence might be a good idea.

'Two years, huh?' Bo eventually commented.

That was what he thought was important? *Seriously?* Men!

'Give or take. It's definitely yours, Bo.'

Remy bit her lip as Bo's fingers tightened around his tumbler. Any more pressure and the glass would shatter in his hand.

'Do you want this child?' Bo asked abruptly.

She thought about lying to him, about putting a brave

face on, but she was too tired to try. 'Mostly. The idea of having a child is all so new and it's still sinking in.'

'Have you considered an abortion?'

Although she'd expected the question, along with the others about whether he was actually the father, a wave of disappointment drifted through her. She might not actively want the child—his child—but she couldn't contemplate doing away with the conglomeration of cells that would eventually become the perfect mixture of him and her.

When she didn't say anything Bo jumped into the conversation. 'Look, if you say this kid is mine, and the tests prove that it is—well, I'll raise it...her...him...if that isn't what you want to do.' Bo rubbed a hand over his face. 'Just don't get rid of it, okay?'

Remy looked astonished. 'Why would I do that?'

'It's been known to happen,' Bo snapped.

Remy saw something pass through his eyes—something under the veneer of calm that suggested deep pain and a healthy dose of panic. She'd given him every possible option to step away from her emotionally, yet he still stood there, processing the situation.

'You're not behaving as I expected you to,' she whispered, trying to contain a yawn. Nobody had so far.

'I never read the manual on how to react when you're told that a one-night stand is pregnant with your child,' Bo replied.

'You're so calm and collected. I expected you to be shouting and swearing.'

'You're pregnant, and you say that I am the father. We can't change that so we have to deal with it.'

'Well, I feel like I've been hit by a two-by-four,' Remy muttered.

'You *look* like you've been hit by a two-by-four,' Bo shot back. He stared down at his whiskey glass. 'Are you expecting me to suggest that we get married?'

Remy's mouth fell open in surprise. 'You're kidding, right?'

Bo just looked at her, his gaze steady.

'Why would you ask that?' Remy demanded. 'I don't *want* to get married!'

'I didn't ask you to. I asked whether you were *expecting* me to ask. Big difference.'

'Why would you even raise the subject?'

'Because some people would think it's the right thing to do.'

'In the last century, maybe!' Remy retorted, flummoxed at the thought of being this man's wife.

What would that be like? she wondered. How would it feel to be able to play with his body day in and day out?

Marriage, she reminded herself, *is more than sex, you moron.*

Marriage—any relationship with a man as strong-willed as Bo—wouldn't be a partnership or anything close to it. If he was anything like the other strong, corporate alpha men she'd met then it would mean that he'd want to control her, harness her. She'd been under her mother's thumb all her life—she wasn't going to swap one type of control for another. She'd never give *anyone* that much power over her in any way: work, personal life or anything in between. It was a vow she had no intention of breaking—ever.

'Are you crazy? I'm not getting married just because I'm pregnant! We don't even *know* each other!' Remy stated emphatically.

Bo just kept looking at her, his expression unreadable and his eyes steady. 'Again, I didn't ask. But I *will* take care of you and the child.'

'I don't need taking care of!' Remy enunciated each word clearly. 'I don't need *anything* from you.'

'Then you shouldn't have bothered to tell me and we could've avoided this conversation.' Bo leaned forward and his eyes pinned her to her seat. 'But you *did* tell me, and I'm not the type of guy who will stand on the sidelines while you make all the decisions about my child's life.'

Remy, not even remotely intimidated, narrowed her eyes. 'This is *my* child and *I* make the decisions. This was a courtesy visit—nothing else.'

'Like hell it was. Do not even *think* about leaving town; I will not be happy if I have to track you down.'

Remy rolled her eyes. 'And how do you intend stopping me?'

'Any way I have to.' Bo placed his empty glass on the table next to him and slapped his knees. He glanced at his watch and stood up. 'I need to make a call, and then I'll take you back to your truck.'

'Yay—because I am *so* over arguing with you,' Remy murmured, her eyes drooping closed. 'You're lucky I'm feeling so tired, because if I weren't I'd be tearing into you for being a high-handed, bossy, arrogant jerk! When I'm feeling better, I will.'

'I'm *so* scared.' Bo's tone was pure sarcasm.

'You should be.' Remy forced her eyes open to glare at him. 'I'll just close my eyes for a minute or two while I wait for you…'

Within seconds she was out like a light.

CHAPTER FOUR

Bo CAST A glance across to his right. Instead of seeing the sleeping passenger he'd expected Remy was wide awake, and those pale eyes, witch-like in the low light of the car's interior, were watching him.

'Slick car.' Remy stated in her sex-on-legs voice.

Bo flicked another glance in her direction and wondered whether he was imagining the note of criticism in her voice. Yeah…the car was German and expensive and fast. He worked damn hard and ran a successful company and he believed he deserved a toy or two. Before Ana had died he'd loved his Ducati, but he hadn't been on his 'Cat' since.

'You have a problem with German sports cars?'

'Not generally. I usually have a problem with the men who drive them,' Remy replied, rubbing both hands over her face. Before he could reply, she held up a hand. 'Sorry… I'm not trying to pick a fight.' Remy blew out another long sigh and looked out of her window as they turned onto the main road to Bellevue. 'So, this must have been a hell of a day for you, huh?'

That was putting it mildly. 'I never expected to see you again and now you're back with a baby. *My* baby.'

That made him wonder, for the hundred and fourth time, how he'd lost control—the control he was so famous for.

'I'm still wrapping my head around the fact that I messed up by not using protection…' He hesitated for a brief moment, blindsided with the hot memory of how incredible she'd felt as he'd slipped into her. He cleared his throat. 'That tiny slip has had far-reaching, life-changing—life-*creating*!—consequences.'

Fate was laughing its ass off at him.

Remy placed the side of head on the window. 'Did you and your wife want kids?'

He never discussed his wife with his lovers—ever. Actually, he never discussed Ana at all. He thought he'd feel resentful and annoyed at her question, but it was just another surprise in a night of surprises that he didn't.

He cleared his throat and managed a one-word response. 'I did.'

He caught the searching look she sent in his direction. He wondered what her reaction would be if he told her that Ana had been vehemently opposed to having children and had casually informed him—on their honeymoon!—that she'd aborted a child shortly after she left college. The lost baby hadn't been his, thank God, but finding out about her antipathy towards children—he thought he knew everything about her—had been a shocking post-wedding present. He'd spent the next six months trying to change her mind but he'd underestimated her stubborness and the issue had driven a wedge between them.

'It must be tough that instead of having a child with the wife you loved you're having one with me—a woman you hoped never to see again.'

Actually, so much had happened tonight that he hadn't really had time to think about that until she brought it up. 'I—'

God, what had he been about to say? That he'd *wanted* to see her again? That he'd thought about her more than he should have? That she'd left an indelible impression on him?

He had—and she did.

Bo pushed a weary hand through his thick hair. Today had been a flip-your-life-over day, a massive turning point. 'It's been…*challenging*. I'm having a child with a complete stranger—a woman I've spent less than twelve hours with.' His glance was filled with irony. 'A woman who seems to be stubborn and independent and iron-willed.'

'That's me,' Remy murmured, her voice free of heat but lacking conviction.

What did *that* mean? That she *wasn't* as independent and strong-willed as she portrayed herself to be? Bo rubbed the back of his neck. He was too exhausted for these mental mind games, he realised.

'You can still walk away from this situation,' Remy reminded him.

'As much as you'd like me to do that, it's not going to happen. If you are carrying my baby, then I'm in this for the long haul.'

His baby…inside her because he hadn't been able to resist the impulse to experience what she felt like without the barrier of latex between them. She'd felt like nothing on earth—amazing—as if he'd come home…

No, home had been *Ana*, he mentally corrected himself.

Despite his frustration with his wayward thoughts Bo shuddered with lust. Ruthlessly he pushed away those hot, sexy, make-him-hard memories.

'*If* I am carrying your baby…' Remy repeated his words. 'You still have doubts that it is yours?'

Logic dictated that he should—that he should be suspicious and wary. He didn't know Remy at all. He'd shared one night with her and for all he knew this could be a mother of a trap. Maybe she'd slept with someone else and was trying to pin it on him. Or she'd slept with a whole lot of guys and thought that he was the best bet for coughing up the dough.

But…

He sighed heavily. *No.*

Just…no.

As much as he would have liked to believe that she was snowing him, he'd seen the truth in her eyes when she'd told him that he'd been her first lover in two years, that he was definitely the father. He knew that he would see the truth in her eyes right now if he looked for it. It was his kid. But she didn't want anything from him and fully intended walking this road alone.

Like hell, Bo thought.

'I believe that I got you pregnant,' Bo said as they entered the outskirts of Bellevue. 'And because I do believe it you should start realising that this is my kid too, and there is no question about whether I want to part of the child's life. I *will* be part of his…her…life.'

The thought was terrifying. And exciting. Of course it was. This baby would be the first of the new generation of Tessiers, and he didn't want his child bouncing from town to town with its free-spirited 'It will all be okay I can do it on my own' mother.

Its free-spirited but *feminist* mother, who didn't seem to grasp the concept of co-parenting or the fact that he would be part of her—correction—part of the baby's life!

His baby would have a home, stability, consistency, immediate and constant access to a parent. All the things he hadn't had as a child. He'd loved his parents, and in their own way they had loved him and Ginny, but they hadn't been a model of responsibility or domesticity. Their own needs and their need to save and uplift the poor, the sick and disadvantaged of the world had come first, and he and Ginny had been supposed to get with the programme and suck it up.

A French school in Equatorial Guinea and they couldn't speak French? Learn! Jumped by a bunch of ten-year-old thugs in a *barrio* in Rio? Fight back! Malaria in Indonesia? Sweat it out!

When it came to child-rearing his parents had believed in the 'toss 'em in at the deep end and make 'em swim' school of thought. They'd sink or they'd swim. Bo had made damn sure that both he and Ginny swam. And the need to protect his loved ones was a childhood trait that had followed him into his adult life and into his marriage.

Children needed stability and protection and roots, and if Remy couldn't provide that—how could she with her vagabond lifestyle?—he would.

He hadn't been able to save Ana from herself. He'd never wanted her to get her own superbike, but she'd wheedled one out of him and riding their powerful machines through the valley had been one of their favourite things to do. Until that day...

He'd warned her—twice!—that she had to slow down in the wet and misty conditions. She hadn't. Which had led to her taking a corner too fast. The bike had slid out from under her and she'd slammed into a concrete barrier. He'd held her in the rain as she slipped away...

Don't go there... Bo snapped his attention back and pulled up in front of Remy's hotel, parking in an empty space and staring up at the pretty façade.

'We need to have a proper talk,' he said, keeping his voice low. 'A serious "let's work this out" talk.'

Remy picked her handbag up off the floor as she nodded. 'I know. Just not tonight.'

No, not tonight. They were both at the end of their tethers and nothing good would come out of discussing this further right now.

Bo pulled in a couple of deep, calming breaths and ran his hand through his hair as he climbed out of his Mercedes to walk around the car and open Remy's door.

She lifted her nose. 'I don't need you to open doors for me.'

He sighed. *God, another argument?* 'Cut the feminist crap, Remy. I'm going to open doors and let you walk into rooms first and pull out your chair. If we have a son, so will he. Get used to it.'

She looked surprised at his crisp response, but she eventually put her hand in his, allowing him to help her from the low-slung car.

Bo kept her fingers linked in his, liking the contact, knowing he shouldn't, but too frazzled to care. He placed his other hand on her hip and watched the attraction flare in her amazing eyes. Standing so close to her, he instantly forgot that they were about to be parents, that she was only back because of the baby, that they didn't know or particularly like each other... He just needed to taste her, to feel her breasts pressed into his chest, her small hands touching his skin.

Pale eyes clashed with his and their mouths were a hair's breadth away from each other...so close. Temptation whirled and swirled and Remy's lids half closed, her chin tipping up as if to encourage him to dip his head, to take a nibble, a bite.

God, he wanted to.

The high-pitched shriek of a car alarm pierced their sexual fog and the moment evaporated. Remy placed her hand on his chest and took a step back, her face morphing from turned on to backing off.

It took a minute for her to speak. 'I think this situation is complicated enough without us adding another layer of crazy.'

Bo rubbed the back of his neck, unable to argue. He still wanted her, but they had far bigger problems to deal with.

'Thanks for the lift.' Remy said. A shrug of her shoulders followed her words. 'But I could've driven myself back here.'

'You would've put yourself in a ditch, you're so tired. I'll make a plan to have your truck delivered in the morning. I'll have the keys left at the front desk.'

Remy yawned. 'Okay. Well…goodnight.'

'We'll talk again in the morning,' Bo assured her, and watched as she walked towards the entrance.

Leaning his hip into the door of his vehicle, he folded his arms and stood there for a long time after she'd disappeared inside. Oh, yeah, they'd talk. She needed to fully understand that he intended to be part of this process and would do whatever he had to.

He'd support her until the child was born—pay her medical expenses, her rent, pay for her food. When the baby arrived they'd renegotiate the future. But for now he had to protect Remy, look after Remy, because by protecting her he was protecting his son or daughter and he wasn't losing again…

He wasn't losing anyone he loved, anybody close or emotionally connected to him.

He wouldn't ever remarry, and he'd couldn't fall in love again, but in a roundabout, crazy way he'd been given the one thing he still craved. That he'd always craved.

A child. A little family. *His* little family. And if that meant dealing with sexy…with Remy…he would.

After all, he kind of needed her.

The next morning Bo stood outside Remy's hotel room door, a bottle of mineral water in his hand. He could do with a whiskey, he thought, sucking the water down. He would be cool, calm and in control. He wouldn't allow her to goad him into an argument, and he sure as hell wouldn't allow her to distract him with her gorgeous face and slim body.

It galled him to admit that even when they'd been talking about her pregnancy yesterday, even when he'd realised that the baby was his, in the back of his mind—and in his pants—he'd known that he still wanted her. That he needed her mouth fused to his, her longs legs around his hips, needed to be inside her again.

Yeah, well, at least you wouldn't get her pregnant this time, moron, he thought sourly.

Replacing the cap on his water bottle, he frowned at the low sound coming from behind her door. Was that a cat he could hear? It was the slightest mewl, the faintest whimper. Knocking on her door, he kept his ears cocked. He didn't hear any movement from behind the door and wondered if she was sleeping. If she was, then what was that noise he'd heard?

Maybe he was letting his imagination run riot… No—there it was again.

Next he heard a faint moan that was decidedly human coming from Remy's side of the door. Without stopping to think he turned the handle—and shook his head when he realised that the door was unlocked. He pushed it open and glanced towards the bed, instantly concerned when he saw that Remy wasn't in it.

Bathroom etiquette be damned… He spun round and poked his head around the half-open door. Remy knelt on the mat in front of the toilet, clutching her stomach. She glanced up at him, her eyes wide, terrified, and awash with tears.

She groaned. 'Go away.'

'Remy? What's the matter?'

'So sick—can't keep anything down,' Remy said in a wobbly voice.

Bo walked out of the bathroom and waited until she was done. When she came staggering out of the bathroom, her hair snarled and her T-shirt barely covering her butt cheeks, he lifted his eyebrows. Her skin was literally green, and there were huge bags under her eyes. She looked gaunt.

And desperately ill.

He immediately grabbed her arm and shoved her towards a chair so that she didn't faint on him again. 'How long has it been since you've eaten? Had something to drink?'

Remy managed a small shrug. 'Not sure. A day? Two?' She lifted worried eyes to him. 'You drove me back last night. Where's my truck?'

'Still parked in the Belleaire parking area. It's safe.' Bo looked around the room, located her suitcase and headed towards it. 'You, however, are not… I think you're dehydrated.'

Remy shook her head. 'Just pregnant. Morning sickness is normal.'

'I'm fairly sure this isn't normal morning sickness!' Bo riffled through her suitcase and pulled out a pair of jeans and a hoodie. Moving back towards her, he opened the zip to the jeans and bent down in front of her to pull them up and over her ankles. 'I have to get you to a hospital.'

'I'm fine. Just let me go to bed.'

Bo tugged the jeans up her thighs. 'Don't be stupid. You're anything *but* fine.'

'But—'

Okay—she was, officially, the most stubborn woman he'd ever met. 'We are *not* arguing about this, Remy. We can do it the easy way or the hard way—your choice.'

'You are insufferably bossy,' Remy told him, dashing her hands across her wet cheeks before taking his hand to help her stand.

He yanked the jeans up and over her butt and gestured to the zip. 'Can you manage to do that?'

'I'm not *completely* useless,' Remy muttered, zipping up and doing up the button.

The jeans hung on her hips, he realised. She'd lost weight—weight she couldn't afford to lose. Yeah, there was no doubt that she needed medical attention. And he'd make sure she got it—immediately.

'Let's go. Can you walk? Or do you need me to carry you?'

Remy started to argue, but then she must have seen something on his face because she nodded.

She walked over to the bed and shoved her feet into a pair of trainers. She groaned as she bent over to tie her laces and wobbled again. Bo cursed again, and put one arm around her back and the other under her knees. He ignored her protestations and concentrated on manoeuvring his way around the bed. Stopping by the table near the door, he nodded to his car keys and cell phone and asked her to grab them.

'Only if you put me down,' Remy said, with a stubborn lift of her chin.

Bo closed his eyes, seeking patience. 'Remy, trust me— you don't want to test me right now. Now, pick up the keys.'

He'd lost her attention on 'trust me'. He could feel her muscles tense against him and felt her heave. He dropped her to her feet and looked down to see her face drain of the last two specks of colour it possessed.

Then she bolted to the bathroom and slammed the door behind her.

Bo grimaced. Nothing about this entire situation was normal, he thought as he waited for her to emerge. Nothing, he suspected, ever would be.

In the ER, a doctor who barely seemed old enough to shave, much less earn a medical degree, prodded and poked her, stuck a needle in her hand and hooked her up to a drip. Then he patted her on the shoulder and told her to wait while the nurses made arrangements to have her transferred to a room on another floor. Then, with an exhausted sigh, he rushed off to deal with the consequences of a multi-vehicle pile-up.

At the end of her bed Bo paced and spent his time speaking on his cell phone. Remy tuned him out and turned her focus inwards. For the first time she concentrated on the burgeoning life that she felt was fading away. She wasn't bleeding—not yet—but she knew that she was in serious trouble. Cradling her stomach with both hands, she started an internal conversation with her unborn child.

After having been so ambivalent before, now she begged her child to start fighting. Despite her unplanned pregnancy, she wasn't a total idiot. She knew that she'd lost a lot of fluid, that she might be dehydrated, and that it might have consequences for the baby. She was run-down and unhealthy, but she hoped—she so *desperately* hoped—that the little soul hadn't given up and decided already that she was a useless mother and was intending on bailing.

Don't let me start bleeding, she prayed.

After shaking her head at the slew of nurses wanting to flirt with Bo, and a trip to Radiology for a sonar scan, she dozed off—only to wake up feeling disorientated. *Aargh!* She was still in a hospital bed, but in a private room, still in her T-shirt, but minus her jeans. She probably looked like a train wreck. So, the past few hours *hadn't* been a horrible dream…

Forcing her tears down, she swallowed as a hawk-nosed man in his late fifties blew into the room, sat on the bed beside her and took her hand. A stern nurse of indeterminate age stood at his shoulder and Bo hovered in the background, his fists stuck in the pockets of his suit pants.

Remy frowned and yanked her hand from the man's. 'Who are *you*?'

'Henry Graham. I'm an obstetrician.'

The nurse leaned forward and Remy noticed the humorous glint in her eyes. 'Also known as God on this maternity ward.'

Dr Graham laughed. 'By everyone except *you*, Sister.'

Remy took a deep breath and forced her panic down. While Dr Graham perused her file and the nurse took her blood pressure and temperature she glared at Bo—because she needed to glare at something and he was there.

Dr Graham raised bushy eyebrows at Remy. 'You're a very lucky young woman, Ms Draycott.'

Bo stepped closer to the bed and Remy bit the corner of her lip. 'The baby…?' she asked, scared to hear his answer.

'Fine. You are severely and chronically dehydrated but the foetus is still there, heart beating strongly.' He grinned. 'Oh, sorry—that's *hearts* beating strongly.'

Remy stared at the Napa Valley's high priest of pregnancy. 'What?'

'Twins. Definitely.'

Remy shook her head, thinking that this had to be one of those jokes the medical profession played on newly pregnant women. 'I'm not having twins.'

Dr Graham tapped his folder. 'According to the sonar scan they did earlier you are.'

Remy shook her head in a series of jerky movements. 'Nuh-uh—this pregnancy is a mistake and there *cannot* be two of them.'

'Our science is pretty good these days. I promise you, it's twins.'

'I *can't* have twins! I don't know what to do with one baby—how will I manage two?' Remy wailed.

Bo took a step towards her and laid a hand on her shoulder. He looked shell-shocked and confused, but his eyes were steady. 'With my help.'

As tempted as she was, she couldn't rely on his help—couldn't rely on him for anything. She'd come here just to tell him that he was to be a father, not for anything more.

He didn't owe her—them—anything! They'd be fine…
They had to be fine!

Besides, like her mother, he had a take-charge personality that instinctively raised her hackles. Yes, he looked like
a male fitness model and had excellent mattress skills, but
that wasn't enough to make up for his caveman personality.

She didn't need him hovering, making decisions for her,
for her baby…*babies*. *She* made the decisions now—she'd
never allow anyone that amount of power again.

But, a little voice deep inside her whispered, *it's kinda
nice and kinda hot that he's stepping up to the plate, taking responsibility. So many men would've run at the first
chance. I've given Bo a lot of chances and he's still sticking.*

Oh, shut up, voice!

Because she felt discombobulated by those unwelcome
thoughts, Remy tossed her hair over her shoulder and
snorted her disbelief. 'Yeah, I can just see you—changing diapers and cleaning up baby drool, doing the early-
morning feed.'

Bo held her eye. 'I will if I have to.'

A part of her—the weaker side of her—wanted to believe him, wanted to curl up in his arms and rest awhile.
But she'd learnt her lesson: give a strong person a little
control and they'd take everything—usually because they
thought they knew what was best for her. She didn't need
to be looked after and propped up. She could *do* this.

Bo, and his bossy attitude could take a hike. Because
the truth was that he was just the man who'd impregnated
her during an admittedly fabulous one-night stand. She
had to think of him that way…

'This is *my* baby,' Remy said, forcing the words out.

'Babies,' Bo enunciated, loudly and clearly, bending
to speak directly in her ear. 'Double. Two. Twice. Dual.
Twins.'

She *wasn't* going to lose control and slap him, Remy told herself, though her hand was itching to do so. *No hitting, Draycott, even if he deserves it!*

She sucked back her temper and tried again. 'The point is that they are *mine*—'

'Then you shouldn't have told me that I'm the father. I don't walk away from my responsibilities.' He pointed at her stomach. '*They* are my responsibility—and so are you!'

'Like hell I am!' Remy shouted.

'You became my responsibility when you fainted at my feet because you're pregnant! With *my* children!' Bo roared back.

His chest was heaving and his cheeks were stained red with temper. His eyes—his beautiful eyes—looked wild. God, he was hot, she thought. Freakin' sexy. If she wasn't attached to a drip, and if Dr Graham and the nurse weren't watching, she'd be all over him right now. Remy touched her tongue to her top lip and watched, fascinated, as the colour in his cheeks died and his eyes filled with lust.

She knew what he was thinking now because she was thinking it too. *Hot kisses, hard hands...*

Oh, dear God, the attraction between them was still as strong as it had been before. This wasn't good, Remy thought. Not good at all!

Dr Graham cleared his throat and tapped his folder against the bed. When she finally managed to drag her eyes from Bo's sexy face to his, she saw that his eyes were dark and very serious.

'You two done?' he asked.

Remy didn't bother looking at Bo. She lifted one shoulder in a tired shrug. 'For now.'

'You are very run-down, Ms Draycott. Your iron levels are ridiculously low, you're dangerously dehydrated, exhausted, and I'm assuming that you are under some stress. You need to stay on that drip for twenty-four hours and then you need to go home and rest. And you need to stop worrying.'

'You've just told me that I'm having twins,' Remy said, trying to keep her voice from wobbling. 'I think I'm entitled to worry.'

'We'll work it out,' Bo told her, his voice low.

Seeing Bo's obstinate expression, Remy decided not to protest any further. In the first place, she was exhausted, and, secondly, she suspected that he could out-stubborn her.

When she was stronger, feeling more like herself, when she could summon all her fake confidence to wage another battle, she'd explain that she didn't need his money, or his overbearing and arrogant attitude. That she didn't need him to take care of her.

She was perfectly capable of taking care of herself...

It was imperative that she kept her distance from him—emotionally and physically. She reluctantly admitted that she was as attracted to him now as she had been before, and she knew that he just needed to kiss her once, to brush that incredible mouth against hers, and she'd be in his arms and his bed again. She was that easy when it came to him, and she had to resist being swamped by lust and attraction. She wasn't going to fall into a physical relationship with the father of her babies.

Creating life together had forged a bond—she had to remain clear-thinking about this. The only reason they had reconnected was because she was carrying his children. He knew less than nothing about her. He knew her body, but nothing of her mind... And she was only useful to him because he seemed to want the children they'd made together.

She was his means to an end—yet another example of being kept around for what she did and not who she was.

She had to be careful of him. He would want to make

all the decisions and she would lose herself, go back to being who she'd been when she'd allowed her mother and her aspirations for her to dictate the course of her life.

No one would ever do that to her again. This wasn't a made-for-TV drama, it was real life—*her* real life. Bo wasn't a hero, and this story wasn't going to have a Hollywood movie ending.

There was nothing between them except some residual sexual attraction and the lives inside her. *They* had to be their focus and nothing else.

Remy shoved her hair away from her forehead and bit the inside of her lip, determined to get back to the matter in hand.

She turned back to Dr Graham and pulled up a tired smile. 'Anything else I need to know?'

'Folic acid, vitamins, lots of iron-rich food. And rest. Wait—let me repeat that: *rest*. I don't want you doing anything strenuous for a week or two. The next few weeks are pretty crucial. If you can get through the first trimester without any more problems, then I think you have a good chance of delivering two healthy babies.'

Dr Graham leaned over and picked up an injection from the tray next to her bed. She whimpered in anticipated pain. But instead of jabbing it into her flesh, as she'd expected, he placed the needle into the valve on her drip.

He tipped his head at Bo. 'No exertion, healthy food, no stress.'

Bo gave him a brief nod. 'I'll make sure that happens.'

'She'll sleep now,' Dr Graham said, nodding to the drip.

Remy wanted to protest at his talking to Bo, to remind them that she was still present…except that her tongue felt thick and her eyelids heavy.

Oh, hello, sleep…missed you so…

CHAPTER FIVE

HE NEEDED A drink, Bo decided, dropping his keys into the bowl on the hall table and his briefcase to the floor. Yanking his tie down, he flipped open the collar on his shirt and quickly rolled his sleeves up to his elbows as he walked into his kitchen and straight to the fridge.

After he'd had a glass of liquid courage he'd take a walk down the passage, knock on the door to his spare room and see if the mother of his—he swallowed his panic in two big gulps—his *children* was awake. Bo rested his unopened beer bottle against his forehead and closed his eyes. He was going to be the father of not one child but two…

Freakin' hell.

Ginny and Eli were going to roll on the floor and laugh their asses off at this latest development. He could almost hear their comments. *When you do something you go overboard!* And, *You take overachieving to a whole new level of ridiculousness.*

After spending most of the night in an uncomfortable chair next to Remy's hospital bed, he'd brought her back to his home early this morning and deposited her, still half-asleep, in the bed in his guest bedroom. Thinking that she'd be fine if he left her to rest, he'd finally made it to his office by the middle of the morning, where he'd struggled to concentrate on the work he needed to plough his way through. He'd never had a problem with focusing before, but at the most inopportune moments Remy's pale face and scared eyes had flashed onto the big screen of his mind and he'd had to resist the urge to hightail it back to his house to check on her.

He'd programmed his number into her mobile and left a sticky note attached to the phone telling her to call him if she needed anything or ran into a problem. He'd also— because he still didn't trust her not to bolt—taken the tote bag containing her car keys and purse with him to work.

He'd probably catch hell for that, but he didn't give a damn… He was *not* going to chase the mother of his twins across the country. She was going to stay put. Even if he had to tie her to the damn bed.

A knock on his kitchen counter had him jumping a foot in the air, and he whirled around to see Ginny standing on the other side of the granite worktop, looking concerned.

'God—give me a heart attack, why don't you?' he growled as his stomach fell back down his throat.

'Sorry…' Ginny slid onto a bar stool and placed her elbows on the counter, holding her face in her hands. 'Bit jumpy, aren't you?'

'No sleep,' Bo replied tersely, lifting his beer bottle in her direction. 'Want one?'

Ginny nodded. 'Listen, before I interrogate you about how you feel about becoming a daddy, I want to tell you something in case I forget…'

Bo pulled another beer out of his fridge and cracked the top on Ginny's, handing it over before opening his own.

'What's up?'

'I went for a bike ride this morning and I cycled over to Bella's Folly, thinking that I'd just check up on the house.' She shrugged and took a sip from her bottle. 'I went in via the path that comes out at the orchard at Bella's Folly and when I hit the orchard I heard voices I stopped behind the hedge and saw a couple of men standing by the back door, peering into the windows of the house.'

Bo narrowed his eyes. Okay, where was she going with this?

'Craig Cowen was there—and Glen Jance.'

'The real estate agent and the property developer…' Bo ran his hand through his hair. 'Dammit, what do *they* want with the property?'

'To bulldoze the house and put up a gated community or a mini-mall?' Ginny shuddered.

He echoed her horror but, as much as he wanted to give this news the attention it deserved, his mind was too full of Remy. She was in his house and the baby that they'd still been wrapping their heads around was now a two-instead-of-one deal.

He forced himself to concentrate. 'We need to discover what their plans might be—try to find out whether they know more about possible heirs to the estate than we do.'

'Basically, it's a race as to who gets to the heir first with a purchase offer,' Ginny mused. 'What happens if we find the heir and he refuses to sell?'

Bo shrugged. 'Let's cross that bridge when we get to it,' he suggested, glancing out through the window to see Eli striding up to the back door, looking hot and sweaty and desperately in need of a beer.

As he stepped into the kitchen Bo tossed him a beer bottle and sent an uneasy look down the passage. Shouldn't Remy be up and awake by now? How long did pregnant woman actually sleep? What if she had started to miscarry since he'd left her earlier that day? What if she'd *died*?

Can you be any more melodramatic, moron?

She was fine. The doctor had said she just needed to rest and take it easy—that she'd sleep a lot for the next couple of weeks while her body adjusted to being pregnant. But what if something had gone badly wrong in the hours since he'd last seen her?

For crying out loud in a freakin' bucket—just go and check already!

Bo slammed his beer bottle on the counter and looked at Ginny and then at Eli. 'I just need to do something and then we'll talk.'

'Well, hello to you too…' Eli said dryly to his departing back.

Remy rolled over and slowly opened her eyes, blinking at her unfamiliar surroundings. The walls to the spacious bedroom were painted in a soft green, the linen was white and luxurious, and the curtains were a deep green.

Expensive, but tasteful, Remy thought on a yawn, and not her hotel room. Knowing that she needed a minute to get all her brain cells firing at once, she sat up on her elbows and yawned again as she mentally rewound. She'd been vomiting… Bo had taken her to the hospital…twins.

Her eyes shot open. Dear Lord, she was having *twins*. Dual…duplicate…two. *Twins*. Holy hell. She was a single mother, expecting twins. *Get used to it,* she ordered herself, and shuddered in good old-fashioned panic. Sucking in air, she forced down the terror and focused on carrying *one* child. One child she could deal with, could plan for. Maybe in a week or two, when she was used to the idea of being a mommy, she could think about how she was going to be the mommy of twins.

The little she'd seen of motherhood didn't inspire her. While travelling she'd spent a *lot* of time watching people, and she'd seen frazzled mothers, tired mothers, teary mothers, irritated mothers—many with husbands and partners trying to help.

Remy swallowed. She would be alone…doing it alone. With twins. *God.* Okay, Bo had said that he'd be there, but the reality was that for the first couple of years, until they became proper little humans, able to walk and talk, the burden of their care would be on *her* shoulders.

Feeling her breath becoming rapidly more shallow, Remy decided to deal with that reality a little later and tried to make sense of the rest of the her life. She'd been dehydrated, placed on a drip for twenty-four hours, then she'd passed out. She had a vague memory of leaving the hospital, of Bo's strong arms lifting her into his low slung silver car.

And that was it… She remembered nothing more.

Remy narrowed her eyes as she sat up, feeling a lot better than she had for a week. Stronger, and more up for a fight—which was excellent news since Bo had essentially kidnapped her!

And, no, she *wasn't* being dramatic. He'd taken her from her hotel room, removed her from the hospital and brought her here—wherever *here* was!

At least he'd had the sense to kidnap her stuff as well, Remy thought as she swung her legs out of bed. Her suitcase stood in the corner and her laptop sat on the pretty desk by the window. No tote bag, though. Hmm, that was annoying. Mr Bossy had probably kept that with him to make sure she couldn't leave Bellevue.

She couldn't blame him… She might have done the same if she'd been in his position. He, like her, was obviously a strategic thinker who liked to scan the horizon for possible problems… That was something she'd have to remember when dealing with him.

Standing up, and happy to see that she'd stopped wobbling, Remy walked over to the window and pulled it open, gasping at the stunning view of vineyards and mountains in the distance.

She was at Belleaire and, if she wasn't mistaken, it was dusk. Her stomach growled and Remy looked down, surprised. How long had it been since she'd eaten? And why was she wearing a soft red T-shirt that hung off her shoulders midway to her thigh?

Remy put her hand under the shirt and touched her pantyless butt. She'd been dressed in jeans and a hoodie when she'd gone to the hospital, so who had undressed her and pulled this T-shirt over her naked body?

She prayed that it had been one of the nurses at the hospital or, at a push, Ginny. She'd just die if Bo had seen her passed out and naked. When had she last shaved her legs, under her arms? Leaning down, Remy ran a hand up her shin and let out a relieved sigh... Not too bad, she thought.

Remy lifted her hand to her hair. She could feel that it was filthy and snarled, and she knew that she needed a long, long shower.

Walking around the bed to the en-suite bathroom, she sighed in appreciation at the luxury within. The spacious room contained a spa bath, a power shower, dual basins, and a basket with a selection of soaps, shampoos, hair conditioners. Flipping on the taps to fill the bath, Remy lifted the various soaps to her nose and decided on the berry-scented range, placing everything she needed on the edge of the tub.

While she waited for the bath to fill she brushed and flossed her teeth and wondered how she was going to handle Mr Sexy-But-Bossy. Now that she'd had a decent night's sleep and was feeling remotely human she had some very hard thinking to do.

And she couldn't think of a better place to do it in that in a spa bath, up to her ears in bubbles.

Tossing in some bubble bath, Remy pulled off the T-shirt and slid into the hot water, pleasure popping along with the bubbles on her skin. An icy glass of Chardonnay would make this experience complete...

That wasn't going to happen for seven months or so—

how was she supposed to have these babies without the
calming powers of the fermented grape?

Okay, thinking time. Let's deal with the twins issue...

'Are you okay?'

'Waaaaa-aaaaaaah!' Remy sat up fast and water and
bubbles sloshed over the side of the tub. She gaped at Bo,
who stood in the doorway to the bathroom, looking hot
and tough and sexy and dishevelled. And, underneath all
that, a little overwhelmed.

Remy tried to pull the remaining bubbles in the bath
so that they covered her breasts—before she realised that
she was stealing the cover for her groin area. Frustrated,
she sank down lower into the tub and crossed her legs at
the highest point they could be crossed, folding her arms
over her nipples.

Bo, the jerk, just walked over to the tub and perched on
the side.

'What are you *doing*?' she squawked. 'Get *out*!'

He raised an eyebrow and lifted his hands in a *what's
the problem?* gesture. 'I've seen it all before.'

'That was *before*! It was different!' Remy sank so low
into the bath that her chin skimmed the water. 'Go away!'

'Stop being ridiculous for a minute and talk to me,' Bo
commanded in that voice that made her itch to slap him.
'How are you feeling?'

'Oooh, let's think about that. Embarrassed that I'm
naked? Annoyed with you? Irritated that you have once
more acted without my permission and brought me somewhere I don't want to be?'

'You're in my spare bedroom—not a cell in Alcatraz,
woman,' Bo growled. 'Stop bitching at me for two seconds
and tell me how you're feeling—physically.'

Remy looked into his eyes, dark and bleak, and saw that
he was beyond tired. His eyes were shadowed in purple
and his mouth was a thin line in his face. *She* might have

had a really miserable time lately, but Bo hadn't been for a casual stroll in the park either.

'I'm feeling a lot better, thank you,' she admitted reluctantly. 'I'm a bit hungry, actually.'

Bo folded his arms across his chest and she had to give him credit for the fact that he kept his eyes firmly on her face. 'I'm not surprised, since you haven't eaten in, like, a *week*. Get out, get dressed, and I'll get some food into you.'

She opened her mouth to argue, to say that she could sort herself out, but stopped when she saw Bo cracking a huge yawn. He'd tensed in anticipation of her argument and lifted his shoulders to his ears. Exhausted and stressed and…*worried*, Remy realised. She could see it in his eyes, in the way that his hand fisted on his thigh.

'Okay, I'll get out and get dressed *and* allow you to feed me—on one condition,' Remy said, keeping her voice low.

Bo closed his eyes in dread. 'Oh, God—what *now*?'

'Can we just not argue? Just for one night can we try to be civil to each other? I don't want to fight…not tonight.'

He looked surprised at her response, and she saw the quick flash of relief on his face. *Good call, Draycott,* she applauded herself. She could argue, fight, defend her corner if she had to, but every warrior needed some downtime. Bo looked drained and exhausted and as if he just desperately needed a solid dose of 'normal'.

So did she.

Bo held her eyes. 'We wouldn't fight if you just did it *my* way.'

His words were inflammatory and she opened her mouth to take up her verbal sword. She was just about to let rip when she caught the teasing glint in his eye. He had the ability to keep his face utterly implacable, but his eyes reflected his soul. It was a good reminder to her to look before she reacted.

'Or if you saw things *my* way,' she countered gently.

Bo reached down and picked up a long strand of hair that had fallen onto her cheek. He pushed it away from her face. 'This would be a lot easier if one of us was the Chief and the other the Indian…me being the Chief, of course.'

Remy sighed as the tips of his fingers drifted across her cheek and flittered over her jawline. It was ridiculous that such a light touch could ignite a fire between her legs. She struggled to keep her brain from shutting down at the mere thought of having him touching her again, making love to her again.

'Honey,' she drawled, 'I'm pretty sure that if I was meant to be controlled I would come with a remote. Now, do me a huge favour—please?'

Bo grinned at her sass before yawning again. 'Mmm? What?'

'Get out so that *I* can get out?'

'But I've seen it—'

Remy splashed water up onto his shirt and smiled when some drops hit his face. Grandma Rosie's favourite saying popped into head and flew out of her mouth. 'Do *not* make me unleash the monkeys, Robert.'

Bo wiped his face with his hand and pulled his wet shirt away from his chest. 'So, are we calling a truce for tonight?'

'Yeah.' Remy flashed him a quick smile as he stood up. 'And as a bonus I'll try not to faint or puke on you.'

'That would be a nice change.'

While they waited for Remy to join them, Ginny told Eli what she'd seen at Bella's Folly and Bo waited for his cousin's reaction.

Shrugging his broad shoulders, Eli took a swig from his bottle of beer and put his sock-covered feet up on Bo's coffee table. 'We need to find that heir—or else we're going to end up with a shopping mall on our doorstep.'

His thoughts exactly. 'I managed to touch base with the PI I hired, but he's hitting dead ends.' Bo rubbed the back of his neck in frustration. 'The only consolation is that if *we're* having difficulties chasing down the heir, then so will anyone else.'

'And we still don't know whether anyone was actually stipulated in a will?' Eli asked.

'*Nada.*'

Bo caught movement out of the corner of his eye and stood up as Remy, dressed in worn jeans and a simple white T-shirt, stepped into the room. Eli lumbered his way to his feet and Remy's gaze flicked from his face to Bo's and then to Ginny's. Her expression was pleasant, but the hands rubbing her thighs told him that she was feeling a great deal more nervous than she looked.

'Hi…' she murmured.

Eli lifted his eyebrows and Ginny, as loving as always, walked across the room to pull Remy into a quick hug. 'How are you? And how's my nephew or niece? What do you think it is?'

Remy pushed her damp hair back from her face and tossed him a quick look. He read the message in her eyes. *This is your family. You get to tell them.*

He knew that Eli and Ginny were curious as to why Remy was in his house and not in the hotel in town. If he didn't explain tonight, then they would both call him later… He might as well kill two birds with one stone.

But first things first.

'Take a seat, Remy. Can I get you something to drink?'

Ginny opened her mouth, obviously to hurl a question at his head, but he quickly spoke over her.

'Remy? Wine? Beer? Something stronger?'

Remy tapped her tummy. 'Sadly, no alcohol allowed— remember? Something soft.'

So *that* was a stupid question, Bo thought as he walked to the kitchen. And stupid was how he would continue to sound if he didn't learn more than he currently knew about being pregnant, which was how to avoid making babies.

The irony of that thought was not lost on him.

If he was going to spend a lot of time with Remy—and he planned to—he was going to have to learn about pregnancy and babies and birth. He'd never had a problem with learning something new, but he'd always figured that he'd missed his chance to experience all this when Ana had died. On his way to the kitchen Bo pulled out his smart phone and tapped out a memo to remind himself to find a couple of books on gestation.

Bo grabbed a carton of juice from the fridge, poured Remy a glass and walked back into the lounge—where his three guests sat in uncomfortable silence.

Bo handed Remy her glass and shook his head. 'She's pregnant—not mute,' he muttered, taking a seat next to Remy on the couch.

'How did you fall pregnant?' Eli demanded. When he heard his own words, quickly followed by derisive looks, he rolled his eyes. 'I mean, I know *how*… What I meant to ask was how did you meet?'

Remy rested her glass on her knee. 'It was supposed to be a one-time thing. I was passing through Bellevue, we met in a bar, did the…the obvious, and that was supposed to be it.' Remy bit her lip. 'I know you guys are surprised that I'm here, in Bo's house, and to be honest so am I.'

Eli and Ginny exchanged a look and Bo thought that it was time he jumped in.

'Remy's been pretty sick. Yesterday morning I went to see her at the hotel and she was very ill. I took her to the hospital and she was severely dehydrated and anaemic. After they discharged her I brought her here…' He saw

Eli's amused expression and frowned. 'I needed to be able to check on her.'

Eli lifted up his hands. 'I didn't say anything.'

Bo scowled at him again. 'Remy needs to take it easy for a while or she runs the risk of miscarrying.'

Ginny looked worried. 'Oh, Remy, that's horrible. Of course you must take it easy, be quiet. The baby's health comes first.'

'Babies,' Bo muttered, exhausted.

'Twins,' Remy added.

There was long silence before Eli's booming laughter filled the room. Bo watched, resigned, as Eli doubled over, tears running down his face.

Remy leaned into his shoulder. 'Why is he laughing?' she asked, perplexed. 'It's really not that funny. Terrifying, yes—funny, no.'

'He's laughing at me,' Bo explained, weary. *Here they come,* he thought as Eli wiped his eyes. *The smart-ass comments. Three, two, one...*

'Overachieving again, dude?' Eli asked. 'Seriously, you don't *always* have to go the extra mile.'

'Shut up, E,' Ginny snapped, her eyes on Remy. 'Twins? Seriously? When are you due?'

Bo rolled his head against the back of the couch, realising that he was as interested in her answer as Ginny. He should *know* the date that his world would be flipped upside down.

'End of March next year. But they say that twins normally come earlier—especially on the first pregnancy.' Remy tapped her finger against her glass before pulling in a big breath.

'Well, that gives you some time to sort things out,' Ginny said prosaically. 'Are you guys getting married?'

Bo was too tired to react to the question but Remy's spine stiffened in... What? Horror? Annoyance? Panic?

She shook her head and looked at him, aghast. 'What *is* it with you lot and the need to get married?'

Bo dredged up a smile and patted her back.

A small frown creased Ginny's forehead. 'So you don't want to get married?'

Remy shuddered. 'Hell, no!'

'Ever? Or not just because you're pregnant?' Eli asked, resting his beer bottle on the arm of his chair.

'I'm not…the type.' She dismissed the subject with a wave of her hand. 'Anyway, to get back to the subject, I just came to Bellevue to tell Bo that I'm pregnant and my life sort of ran away from me.'

'Big-time,' Ginny agreed. 'How long are you going to be in town for now?'

Remy turned her head and her pale eyes met Bo's. He was as interested as his sister was, so he just lifted his eyebrows and waited for her answer.

'A couple of days. Bo and I need to talk through a couple of things and then I'll leave.'

'Not gonna happen,' Bo stated, not willing to let that comment go. She didn't know it yet, but she was staying right where she was—probably for the next eighteen years at least.

Remy turned in her seat and scowled at him. 'What? Are you going to kidnap me again?'

'If I have to.' Bo shoved his hand into his hair and sighed. 'We're arguing—we said we weren't going to do that tonight.'

Bo thought he heard a soft curse word before she pursed her lips. He knew that she was considering whether to carry on arguing or to let him have the last word.

She opened her mouth, closed it again, and then pouted. 'Dammit. We *did* agree to that.'

Bo thought he'd push his luck. 'We also agreed that I was the Chief and you were the Indian.'

Remy patted his knee, the action condescending. 'You're having delusions again…maybe they should up your medication?'

Remy curled herself into the corner of Bo's comfortable couch, feeling sleepy and full after an excellent meal delivered from the renowned restaurant on the estate. It had been a simple steak, potatoes *au gratin* and fresh garden vegetables, but beautifully cooked and presented. It had been exactly what she'd needed and wanted to eat, and for the first time in days she felt vaguely normal. Well, as normal as a highly educated, homeless pregnant vagrant could feel.

She needed a day or two of rest, good meals, some light exercise and then she felt that she'd be able to face her future and make some decisions. She'd reluctantly spend another night in Bo's spare bedroom, but then she'd move back to the hotel or into cheaper accommodation in town. She couldn't stay here…with him…

Remy looked at Bo, who was sitting at the opposite end of the couch she was on, deep in conversation with Eli. Although he still looked played out, she noticed that those broad shoulders had dropped, that his normally hard jaw had relaxed and that his eyes weren't so wary and distant.

These were his people—his rock, his north star. Over dinner she'd listened to them talk and she knew that the three shared an unbreakable bond. The Three Musketeers' motto of 'All for one, one for all' could be their rally cry.

If they had to play the characters in a movie then Bo would be the distinguished Athos—intelligent, handsome, brave but emotionally tortured. Enjoying her game, Remy looked at Eli, so blond and movie-star good-looking. He would have to be d'Artagnan—intelligent as well, but ambitious and crafty and a little…or a lot…naughty. Ginny would be the female version of Aramis, supposedly under their protection—which was an illusion she allowed her cousin and brother to have.

Ginny might be the size of a pixie, but her eyes radiated determination and a warrior spirit and she saw herself as the protector of her family. Because she was carrying Bo's babies Remy had been pulled under her mother-hen wing, and Ginny had given her the third degree about the state of her health, the babies' development, whether she was taking the vitamins and supplements she should be taking.

Bo was hard enough to deal with, but she suspected that he was an amateur compared to Ginny. Remy was surprised that she didn't feel more irritated or scratchy at Ginny's interrogation. Her mother and grandmother—independent, self-contained feminists—had been her sole female relationships in life, and it was disconcerting to realise that maybe she had missed out on something special by keeping herself to herself.

It was nice that her babies would have an aunt who was already halfway in love with them and an adult cousin in Eli who would, she presumed, like them too. If anything happened to her—God forbid—they would have a solid support base.

Did Bo realise how lucky he was to have the complete and utter support of his family? They were going to stand by him come hell, high water and twins—and had no intention of being relegated to the sidelines. The Tessiers stood together. Eli and Ginny liked her, but if she messed with Bo the gloves would come off.

The father of her babies might be a hard-ass—a hard-bodied and hard-eyed man who ran a successful enterprise—but these two people were solidly in his corner, willing to take on the world for him.

Remy shivered as a ghost walked over her grave. Nothing was going to happen to her... Women all over the world delivered healthy twins with no problems at all. Nothing would go wrong. She was just being fanciful and imaginative. But she couldn't help wrapping her arms around herself to counter the sudden drop in temperature.

Bo stopped halfway through his sentence and frowned at her. 'Are you okay?'

Remy nodded and held out her arm, showing him that her skin was covered in goosebumps. 'Just suddenly freezing cold.'

Bo immediately reached for the chenille throw behind his back. He stood up, shook it out and draped it around Remy's shoulders. Remy thanked him, and didn't miss the long, intense look Eli and Ginny shared.

Bo immediately leaned away from her. 'We need to talk about Bella's Folly.'

Ginny must have seen the confusion on Remy's face because she held up a hand to halt their conversation and fill her in. Happy to think of anything else but the rabbit hole she'd fallen into, Remy listened intently.

A strategically positioned house and land, no heir, sharks circling… Her analytical brain kicked in and she leaned forward, intrigued.

'Did she die intestate?' she asked.

Bo lifted a shoulder. 'We think so. Maybe…'

Remy sucked in her bottom lip. 'So the nearest relative inherits…?

'Except that it seems she didn't *have* any relatives. If that is proved to be true, then the state inherits, and dealing with the state is a headache of magnificent proportions,' Remy mused. 'So it would be in your best interests to find someone related to her?'

'Essentially,' Bo agreed.

Remy ran through the possibilities in her head. 'You could hire a private detective.'

'Done that, and they didn't find anyone.'

Okay, Remy thought, that was Plan A. The alphabet

still had another twenty-five letters to attach to a plan. It wasn't the end of the road.

'What about a genealogist?'

Bo and Ginny and Eli were silent for a minute before Bo spoke again. 'I didn't think of that.'

Ginny wrinkled her nose. 'What exactly do they do?'

Remy linked her hands around her bent knee. 'Essentially they trace family trees. If they have a social security number they can trace anyone. They look at birth certificates and death certificates, church records, state records, and piece together who she was, who her relatives were.' Remy looked from one interested face to another. 'I dabbled with it in college. It's mostly computer-based work.'

Of course with *her* computer skills, she could have the information for them in a day…two at the most.

Eli placed his foot on his opposite knee. 'Where would we find a genealogist?'

Should she offer her services? Should she reveal that much about herself? It would mean exposing herself and what she did—had done—and she wasn't ready to do that. Not just yet. Let *them* try the genealogist route, and if it didn't pan out then she might suggest that she have a go. Maybe…

'I know someone in Portland. He's a friend of the family and does this as hobby. Or you could find a firm that does it as a business, but they charge enormous fees if they do it for an outside party. When they look for an heir *they* usually approach the heir, and before they tell him or her what they might inherit they negotiate a percentage of the estate as their fee before they divulge any information. Either way, they take their pound of flesh.'

Bo looked at her as if she'd turned into a arachnid wearing ballet shoes. 'How do you know all this?'

The man obviously thought that because she was a traveller she didn't have a brain in her head. She tossed her head and sent him a chilly smile. 'I have a mind for trivia.'

She did. She also had a mind for maths and statistics and computers and code and science and art and cooking and literature... Being put in a box raised every hackle she had. And she was certain Robert Tessier liked his boxes; they kept his world orderly and in control.

'So you're not just a pretty face?' Bo murmured softly.

You have no idea, Remy thought, not bothering to respond to his dry comment. Bo was very used to being the smartest person in the room, she realised, but he was in for a wake-up call—because she was, without blowing her own trumpet, easily his equal.

As Ginny, Bo and Eli continued with their discussion about finding a genealogist Remy pulled back from the conversation and thought that dealing with Bo was going to be interesting. One of these days they would go head-to-head, and it would be interesting to see who would be the victor—or, if there wasn't an outright victor, who walked away with the least scars.

She could tangle with Bo on a mental level, in fact she'd relish the opportunity to do so. But if they got physical—if he touched her—she knew that she would lose any battle that took place between the sheets. He demanded control there, and she was happy to hand it over to him, knowing that he would reward her with indescribable pleasure.

She couldn't allow him that much control over her— couldn't allow him to see the chink in her armour. It would be risking too much for her to give him that much power over her, and she suspected it was a slippery slope downhill from there. If she gave the man an inch he'd end up taking everything—and there was no way she'd ever allow that to happen.

Remy rested her head against the couch and allowed the conversation to drift over her, feeling bone-deep tired again. And everyone said that pregnancy was supposed to be the *easy* part of motherhood...

She'd had the whole thing planned, Remy thought, picking at a thread on the seam of her jeans. She had genuinely believed that after she'd come back to Bellevue and told Bo she was pregnant she would be able to resume her travelling—at least for a few more months. In that time she'd find a town to settle down in, and while she grew bigger and adjusted to life in a new town she'd start making plans for a business she could start. When she'd given birth she'd have let Bo know and maybe, if he wanted, sent him a picture or two.

Instead she'd found that the father of her babies had an overdeveloped sense of responsibility and wanted to be a part of his children's lives! She had been going to raise this child—children...*eep!*—alone, and now she had to think about how she was going to accommodate Bo into that plan. She wished she could dismiss him from her life and do her own thing but she couldn't—that wouldn't be fair. He had a right to know his children and his children had a right to know him.

And even though leaving Bellevue was still part of her plan she knew that it wasn't sensible, given her health and the fact that she was experiencing a high-risk pregnancy, to leave just yet. While she felt better, she still didn't feel a hundred per cent, and her babies were at risk for the next couple of months. She had to stay put—close to medical care. It would be foolish and stupid to keep travelling; what if she threatened to miscarry and she was in a small town with inadequate medical facilities? She was a free spirit— she wasn't an idiot.

But at the very least she needed to leave his house and move back to town. Because she didn't completely trust herself not to throw herself at him and ask him for a repeat experience of that magical night six...nearly seven weeks ago. He'd kissed like a dream, Remy remembered on a huge yawn, and his big hands had been gentle but demanding. His voice, always deep, had rumbled over her skin, and in itself had been able to stoke her passion. He'd had more than a few tricks up his sleeve and she'd love to know if he had any more…

Remy felt herself sliding into sleep, and was jerked back when big hands and strong arms scooped her up and held her against a hot, broad chest. Sighing, she instinctively looped her arms around his neck and nuzzled her face into his neck, breathing in the faint notes of his aftershave. He was so big and stable and…*solid*, she thought.

'C'mon, Pocahontas, let's get you to bed.'

CHAPTER SIX

REMY WAS SITTING at the kitchen table the next morning, her tablet next to her plate. It tugged at his heart to find her hunched over a piece of dry toast, a cup of herbal tea at her elbow, looking slightly green.

Wanting a minute to catch his breath, Bo hovered outside the kitchen door, his chest heaving after his habitual early-morning run. Bellevue was looking at its best, with the oak trees that lined the long driveway turning green to gold, gold to scarlet. The grass in the fields was still green, the white pole fences had been freshly painted by Ginny's staff, and the air was crisp and clear and that particular blue that was so intense he wanted to shove his fist through it.

Remy had shoved her fist into her sternum and was taking deep breaths when Bo stepped into the room. 'Morning sickness again?'

Remy snapped her head up and managed a wan smile. 'Yeah. Not so bad as before, but still there.' She tapped the tower of three books on the table and sighed. 'These all say it should stop at three months, but—' She shrugged.

Bo resisted the urge to run his hand over her tangled curls and headed for the coffee pot instead, glancing at the books in a pile. 'They're all the same book.' He frowned. 'Why do you have three copies of the same book?'

Remy's grin hit her eyes. 'Your sister. One for you,

one for me, one for her and one for Eli. She ordered them shortly after I fainted in the bistro.'

Bo closed his eyes. 'Typical Ginny. She might give us all a quiz occasionally. Although you'd have to put a gun to Eli's had to get *him* to read it.'

'I realised that.' Remy leaned back in her chair. 'I like Ginny. She has a good…heart.'

'She really does,' Bo agreed. 'She's the best of us.' Bo gestured to the coffee machine. 'Do you want coffee?' Judging by her instinctive grimace he figured that was a no.

'Sorry. It's the smell: coffee, meat frying, onions… But don't let me stop you.'

And have her hurling all over his kitchen floor? Nah, he wouldn't take the chance. So he headed to the fridge and grabbed orange juice instead.

'It's not a problem. I probably drink too much coffee anyway. Try and eat your toast—you need something in your stomach.'

Bo reached for a glass and, dumping it on the table, poured the juice and snagged a bunch of grapes from the colourful bowl of fruit in the centre of the table.

Remy lifted her foot up onto the seat of the chair and rested her forearm on her knee.

Bo pulled out a chair, flipped it back to front and rested his arms on the top strut. 'So, do you want to chat?'

Remy looked at the huge clock on the wall. 'Aren't you in a hurry to get to work?'

He looked at the huge simple clock. Seven-forty. 'I can be late. It's one of the perks of being the boss.'

'Okay…shall I start?'

Bo nodded, and watched as Remy stared down at the table, obviously gathering her thoughts. Eventually she lifted her face up to look at him. Her amazing eyes looked troubled and a little scared.

'I'm still taking all this in, Bo. I thought I would come here, tell you that I was pregnant and then keep travelling.'

'That's not going to happen,' Bo growled, and then he lifted his hand. 'Sorry…sorry. Carry on.'

Remy pursed her sexy mouth and his pants suddenly got tighter. Inexplicably, his excitement just increased when she flashed him the evil eye. But instead of escalating the fight she just sighed and carried on speaking in a normal voice.

'I didn't expect to get so sick, or for you to be so interested in being part of the babies' lives. So I'm really struggling to figure out what to do.'

'Stay here.'

'You make it sound so easy.'

'It is.' Bo popped a grape into his mouth.

'Define "here". Here, as in at your house—or here as in Bellevue?'

'Either. Both.' Bo ran a frustrated hand through his hair.

'For the pregnancy or for the rest of my life?'

Bo knew that if he told her she wouldn't be going anywhere soon he'd lose her, and that they'd end up having a huge shouting match that would solve nothing. No…as much as he wanted to be a control freak dictator, he knew that he'd be making this process so much harder than it needed to be. He had to be smart and strategize his way through this… Remy, unlike Ana, was a woman who made her own decisions.

And that wasn't meant in any way to malign either woman. They were just so damn *different*. Despite Ana's recklessness and always confident if slightly bohemian attitude, underneath she'd been so very insecure and had always looked to him for answers. Looking back, it had sometimes irritated the hell out of him. Sometimes, especially when he'd been stressed and busy, he'd wished that she'd just take the initiative and make the decision—

whether it was a weekend away or new curtains for their bedroom. But she'd always craved his approval and a part of him wondered if her antipathy towards children had been rooted in the fact that she hadn't wanted to share his attention with them. *Unfair, Tessier, cut it out.*

Remy, on the other hand, needed nobody's permission to do anything. She was strong and independent and a little wild... And he knew that her inability to consult would irritate him—*did* irritate him.

He just couldn't win.

But right now he had to win this battle—not the whole war.

Bo sipped his juice and kept his expression pleasant. 'Why don't we take it...? What's the word for parts of a pregnancy?' He looked at the pile of books and snapped his fingers. 'Terms...?'

'Trimesters?'

'That's it. Why don't we take it trimester by trimester?' Bo rested his chin on his fist. 'The doc said that this trimester is dangerous, that you should be careful. You're—what?—eight weeks now?'

'Seven and a bit,' Remy agreed.

'So, I *suggest*—' he emphasised the word 'suggest' '—that you stay with me, here, for the next four or five weeks, until the danger period passes. I can keep an eye on you and be around if you run into problems.'

Remy cocked her head, deep in thought. 'And after that?'

Bo shrugged. 'We have another conversation and see where we are.'

Remy tapped her finger against her cheek. 'What if I can't see myself staying here, Bo? What if this isn't my town? My spot? What then?'

He wanted to shout that it *was*—wanted to tell her that there was no way in hell he could comprehend any arrangement that wouldn't have him seeing her—correction—seeing *his children* every day of his life. But he held back, knowing that if he uttered any of the above he would lose all the ground he'd gained.

It took a massive amount of willpower for him to look casual, to put a reassuring look on his face. 'Trimester by trimester, Remy. We'll cross that bridge when we come to it.'

He'd blow the freaking bridge up if he had to. But she didn't need to know that.

'Concentrate on the next couple of weeks and then we'll chat again. What do you say?'

Remy looked out of the kitchen door and down the passage. 'I don't know if me living with you is a good idea. I think I should move back to town.'

'Why?'

A blush stained Remy's cheekbones. 'I don't want to… to inhibit your…um…social life.'

Social life? What was she going on about? He didn't *have* a social life—hadn't had a sex life since she'd whirled into and out of his life nearly two months ago… Oh, so *that* was what she was asking: whether he had someone who would be upset that she had moved in.

'I'm not seeing anyone, Remy. Haven't seen anyone since you.'

Was that pleasure and a feminine self-satisfaction he saw flashing in her eyes? Nah, it couldn't be. Being pregnant with twins and her resultant sickness had probably wiped the hectic sexual chemistry between them from her mind. Pity… Because, pregnant or not, she was still the only woman he could imagine in his bed.

And that would be the worst idea in the world…

He couldn't complicate this indescribably complicated situation any more by throwing sex into the mix. But he suspected that was a great deal more easily said than done, since she just had to breathe to start the celebration in his pants.

God, this was going to be torture...

Remy chewed her last piece of toast, swallowed, and picked up her tea cup. When she blew out a long breath he knew that he had her.

'Okay, we'll do it your way for the next few weeks and then we'll re-evaluate. But I have a couple of conditions....'

Of *course* she did. *What* a surprise. 'Uh-huh? And what would they be?'

'Have you hired someone for the bistro yet?'

Her left-field subject-change had him scrambling to catch up. He frowned. 'It's on my long list of things to do. Why are you asking?'

'I'll go mad with nothing to do for the next month or so, and I did tell Ginny and Eli that I would help you guys decide on a menu for the bistro.'

Okay, her words were in English but she wasn't making any sense. 'Whoa—back up...explain. You're a *chef*?'

Remy explained how she had met Eli and Ginny in the diner and their discussion about the type of food they wanted to serve. Bo recalled Ginny mentioning having met someone who would be perfect for the position but he'd never considered that it could be Remy. Why *would* he? It was just another reminder of how little he knew of the mother of his children.

He really needed to do an internet search on her, to find out as much as he could, because he knew that he didn't have the patience to wait for Remy to dole out bits of information.

'No, I just know a lot about food. I blog about it and I love to cook. I told them that I would cook some sample dishes, help you guys decide on a menu...maybe design some menus for you.'

Remy gnawed on her bottom lip and he wanted to soothe it with his tongue. *Concentrate, Tessier.*

'I don't expect an answer now—think about it. If you say no I'll find something else. If you don't want me involved with Belleaire business maybe I'll do some waitressing.'

'You told me that you are a shocking waitress.'

'I'm not that bad. I was flirting with you.'

Bo smiled at her, remembering the sassy girl in the bar who'd literally stolen his breath away. 'You did that really well.' He shook off the memories and mentally pulled back. 'I'm not crazy about you working—not after what Dr Graham had to say. Especially waitressing…being on your feet all day. You just need to rest—and that includes not worrying about money. If you give me your banking details I'll transfer some money into your account as soon as I get to work.'

Remy looked at him as if she'd just found out he had a penchant for wearing red lacy underwear. 'You're joking, right?'

Bo held her eye.

'I don't need money—I need to *do* something. If I stay here then I need to do something to repay you for my food and board. I'm not staying here for free.'

'You're having my children, getting ill for them, it's not a problem and it's the least I can do.'

Remy lifted that stubborn chin. 'It is a problem for me. I don't take charity.' She stood up and pushed her chair back. 'I think it's better that I just go back to town, find a place to rent.'

Bo sat up and looked at her straight back, saw the tension in her neck, in her shoulders. She didn't know how to fight, he thought on a moment of clarity. Her default course of action was to remove herself from the argument and go it alone, to do her own thing. Yeah, well, *that* had to change.

'Remy, we are going to have children together. We're going to have to start learning to deal with each other to work things out. We've got at least twenty years ahead of us doing that, and nothing will be accomplished if we walk away from a discussion when it gets tough.'

She'd kept her back to him, but he could tell by the tilt of her head that she was listening.

'Come back, sit down, and let's work this out.'

She kept on staring out of the window but after a long, long time turned around and folded her arms across her chest. 'You're the father of my children, Bo, but your responsibility doesn't extend to me. I will take care of myself in every way that counts. And there is no way in *hell* that I am going to live in your house, eat your food and use your utilities without paying for them or at the very least earning my way. I will *not* sacrifice my independence—financial, emotional and mental—for anybody or anything!'

Whoa! Okay, then, Bo thought, astounded by her vehemence. Someone had done a number on her head. 'It's just money, Remy. I'll make more tomorrow.'

'It's *your* money, Bo, and I won't take it. I wish you would realise—accept—that you are *not* responsible for me.'

He could be—would be happy to be, if she'd let him. He was thirty-five years old. Wasn't it time he started being responsible for someone? Why not Remy?

'But I *am* responsible for those lives you're carrying, and because of that I want to make your life as easy as possible. I have the money to do that, but you have more pride than Lucifer himself.'

Bo stood up, walked across the kitchen and threw the grape stalks into the bin. Money was a tool, he thought, frustrated. What was the point in having the stuff if he couldn't make life easier for those he cared about? He could spend it all, lose it all, and he'd shrug his shoulders, put his shoulder to the wheel and make some more. Being poor didn't scare him, and being rich didn't define him—so why wouldn't she let him use it to make a difference? She was carrying *his* family, which should count for something.

He turned to look at her and held her hot gaze. 'I intend to pay for everything you need.' He saw her face tighten and cursed his choice of words. 'I would *like to* pay for everything—' he amended '—for you and for the kids.'

Remy bit her bottom lip and shook her head. 'I can't let that happen.'

Yeah, *that* was a surprise. Bo threw up his hands. Why not? He had the space, the money, the ability to help her. Why was she being so stupidly proud? And why was he feeling so stupidly annoyed? Horny, frustrated, annoyed… and horny. *God.*

Remy looked at him, her pale eyes steadfast. 'Getting back to our original discussion: I need to do something apart from thinking of these babies. If I don't I'll go mad.'

When she looked at him like that, vulnerable and a little fragile, he'd give her the whole damn world if she asked for it. What the hell…? He needed someone at the bistro and she was here.

'Okay—sure. Do some sample menus for us. I'll pay you an hourly rate.'

'I'm staying here, and if you feed me I'll do it for free.'

Aaargh! Stubborn! He needed a shower. A cold, hard shower. And possibly also a frontal lobotomy to remove the indefinable, churning, volatile emotions he felt whenever he got within twenty metres of this ruddy woman.

Way past time to change the subject—especially since he wasn't winning the argument. He'd have to find another way around her pride.

'There was a message on my machine from the obstetrician's office: you have a follow-up appointment tomorrow at ten.'

Remy grimaced before nodding. 'Okay.'

'I'm coming with you. I want to look at my boys.'

She opened her mouth, no doubt to argue with him, but abruptly changed her mind. 'There might be a daughter in there somewhere,' Remy pointed out, her hand spread across her lower stomach in a protective gesture that rocked his stomach. Her eyes flashed with humour. 'There might be *two* girls in there.'

Good God, he didn't know if he could handle that. 'Girls are complicated…and emotional, irrational. Difficult. I need *boys*, Remy.'

Remy grinned. 'Pigtails, tears, hugs, make-up, PMS, boyfriends, weddings…'

Bo sighed and closed his eyes. Walking over to her, he bent his head to speak into her stomach. 'Take pity on me, guys. Your mother is enough of a handful all on her own.'

'Ha-ha—funny,' Remy said as he stood up.

Bo ran a finger down her cheek, resisting the urge to pull her into his arms, to push his chest into her soft breasts, to slide his thigh between her bare legs, to taste that amazing mouth again, to see her eyes fog over from the pleasure he could give her.

Complicated, he reminded himself.

'I thought so.' He couldn't resist drifting his thumb across her full bottom lip. 'If I tell you to get some more rest, will you argue with me?

'Not today—and not about that,' Remy murmured.

Miracles, Bo thought as he walked away, actually did happen.

Bo and Remy sat in front of Dr Graham's desk and sent nervous looks at the plastic model standing on the corner of his desk. Judging from the box leaning against the wall, Remy knew that it was a called a 4D Pregnancy Pelvis, complete with a baby nestled into the sawn-off uterus. It was fascinating…and slightly gross.

Bo leaned forward and tapped the plastic baby, which promptly rolled out and hit the desk with a loud thump.

Remy giggled. 'You just dropped it on its head.'

Bo picked up the plastic model, looked at it, and slotted the infant back into its cradle. 'It's a puzzle for doctors.' He cocked his head. 'It looks a bit crowded in there—where would the other one go?'

Remy looked down at her still flat stomach and back to the model. 'I don't have a clue.'

Bo leaned back in his chair and placed his ankle on his opposite knee. 'I don't have twins in my family. You?'

Remy thought for a minute. 'I think a great-aunt of mine had twins.'

Bo half smiled. 'So you falling pregnant with twins is *your* fault?'

Remy bumped her elbow into his side. 'I'll cop to the twins if you cop to the fact that you took your time putting on a condom!'

'I don't recall you stopping to remind me,' Bo shot back.

True… She'd been so utterly lost in what they were doing, lost in *him*, that she hadn't noticed. And he had been the thinking one—he'd been the one to remember to cover himself. If it had been up to her… Remy released a long, hot sigh. She would be pregnant. Oh, wait—she *was* pregnant! With twins!

She slapped her hands across his chest. 'If you hadn't leaked…'

'If you hadn't wiggled…'

Bo's eyes were hot on hers. They looked like heated aluminium when he was turned on, she thought, and seeing the passion in his eyes, seeing his desire for her—despite their current craziness—sent heat to her womb and caused her to clench her legs together. She knew that her nipples were on display, and she could feel a hot flush cross her chest, slide up her neck.

She could jump him right here and right now.

And she knew that he would let her.

Her pregnancy had done nothing to dampen the electric attraction between them.

Dammit.

'We can't.' Remy forced the words out, leaning backwards to keep herself from slapping her mouth on his. 'Too, too complicated for words. We have to be sensible about this, Bo.'

Bo tightened his jaw but his eyes didn't leave hers. 'I know…' he growled.

He dropped his leg and leaned forward and Remy got a quick view of the steel-hard erection tenting his pants.

'We're going to be parents together, we're currently living together, yet we're practically strangers.'

'We *are* strangers,' Remy insisted.

'You and I, in any combination, are an accident waiting to happen.'

He sounded as if he was trying to convince himself as well as her, Remy thought. He wasn't doing a particularly good job either.

'And we have the proof.' Remy patted her stomach. 'Which is all *your* fault.'

She added the last comment deliberately, knowing that her accusation would lighten the mood and hopefully break the sexual tension between them. If he kept looking at her like that—as if he wanted to lick her from top to toe and back up again—she was going to accost him in front of the plastic baby.

'You. Wiggled.' Bo enunciated the words clearly.

'I see that you two are still at it?'

Remy snapped her head round and saw Henry Graham standing in the doorway, his shoulder leaning into the door frame and an amused smile on his face.

'How long have you been standing there?' she demanded.

'Long enough.' He strode into his room, slapped a folder onto his desk and frowned at the plastic model. 'Have you two been playing with my pelvis?'

Remy giggled. 'Bo dropped the baby on its head, Dr Graham.'

'Snitch…' Bo muttered.

'Call me Henry—and let's hope he does better with the real thing.' Henry jerked his head to the bed in the corner. 'Talking of the real thing, let's go have a look.'

That evening, while Remy whipped up a quick Thai curry, Bo showed Ginny and Eli his fuzzy photograph of the babies. She had her own photograph, tucked into the back pocket of her jeans, but she couldn't make out much. Bo could point out the heads and the hearts.

Yep, he'd definitely been the one paying attention in class.

'Was it amazing, seeing them, Bo?' Ginny asked, her eyes shining with excitement.

Bo took a moment to reply. He flicked her a glance and their eyes collided. 'Yeah,' he replied gruffly, and she could hear the emotion in his voice.

Amazing, Remy thought, testing the word. Why didn't she feel that? It was weird that everyone, even Eli, was so much more excited than her. What was wrong with her that she couldn't yet feel love or excitement or joy? Was she that emotionally retarded? That selfish?

Maybe it was because she'd never been particularly maternal—had never spent much time around kids or thinking about being a mom. In fact the thought of having children scared her—a lot. What if she was as driven, as demanding as *her* mother? She didn't want to be a pushy mom, but that was what she'd known, what she'd been taught.

She still couldn't get her head around twins. And if she couldn't wrap her head around how she was going to cope with *one* baby, the thought of two had her breaking out in a cold sweat. Two would mean double everything: from diapers to formula, childcare fees, clothes, transport—everything. Two would cost more both financially and emotionally. Two would be double the work, double the struggle, double… Damn, double *everything*.

She couldn't do this. She really couldn't.

She shut off the gas, dropped the spatula and escaped through the open kitchen door and into the cool night. Wrapping her arms around her stomach, she skirted the house and headed for the guest house. Slipping up the dark steps, she sat on the swing bench in the far corner and looked out over the land.

Her life was utterly out of control.

She was staying in Bo's house, cooking for Bo's family and having Bo's babies. She was even about to start working for Bo. She felt as if there were a million ropes tying her to Bellevue and to Belleaire, and obviously to Bo. She didn't like it. She hadn't been tied to anything or anybody for so long.

Remy pulled the band out of her hair in an effort to ease the headache pounding the back of her skull. There was no getting away from it. She was going to be tied to Belleaire and Bellevue and the Tessiers—especially Bo—for a hell of a long time.

Remy felt her heart pound and realised that she wasn't inhaling enough air. She hadn't had a panic attack for years, but if she didn't calm down and get a grip she was going to lose that battle—and soon. She had to regulate her breathing…and her thoughts.

'Let's take it trimester by trimester,' Bo had said.

She had to do that, she realised. She couldn't think further than the next three months. If she did she'd be a basket case before the kids were even born.

You're pregnant—just think about that for now, she told herself.

Remy pursed her lips and recounted what she knew and had read of pregnancy. Weight gain, stretch marks, possible incontinence, blotchy skin, droopy boobs. Hers weren't too bad at the moment—still perky and definitely fuller—but after breastfeeding twins—the better option, according to Ginny's pregnancy book—she was bound to have long, thin, desperately droopy boobs that reached halfway to her crotch.

She'd never get laid again. Even if she had time after the birth she doubted she'd have the energy. And, realistically, what man—Bo—would be attracted to a thin, worn-out, irritable woman with stretch marks, yellow-tinged skin and boobs that functioned as a dairy? Even if she did get a man—Bo—into her bed by force, drugs or bribery, she'd have to interrupt proceedings halfway through to go and pee!

There was no other solution. She'd have to have a hot and torrid affair before she became too gross and too... *mumsy.* Which meant, realistically—since she had the equivalent of two voracious locusts growing inside her—some time in the next month or two. Hmm... Who could she consider? *Ooh, big surprise,* she thought sarcastically, *what about Bo? He's only been constantly on your mind since you met him.*

Except that she really believed what she'd told him the other night: sleeping with Bo would be a colossal mistake. He was going to be part of her life for the *rest* of her life. It would be a lot simpler, a lot smarter, to keep their sexual escapades to one night.

'You okay?'

That would be a *no*, Remy thought, and blinked as her eyes focused on his face. He looked big and tough, but his remoteness was softened by the concern in his eyes. It killed her. She could cope with his sarcasm and his irritation and his brusque attitude, but when this taciturn man displayed his softer side she wanted to fall into his arms and allow his strength—mental as well as physical—to hold her up.

Bo placed his hands in the back pockets of his worn jeans. 'What on earth were you thinking about? You were miles away.'

'Sex,' Remy said, her eyes filling with tears.

If she hadn't felt so wretched she would have been amused by the shock on his face.

'What the hell…?'

'I was thinking about sex, Bo. And that my boobs will drop and my…you know…will stretch, that I'll have ugly stretch marks from the weight gain and that nobody will ever fancy me again!'

I want you so much but I can't have you again. I want to feel sexy and pretty and have you look at me like you did before, with lust and passion and heat. Now I'm just an incubator for your chicks.

Tears that she hated but couldn't stop rolled down her face.

Bo looked at her, utterly perplexed by her sniffles and sobs. He blinked. 'I have no idea what to say except that you're being ridiculous!'

Remy's sobs grew louder, and the more she tried to stop crying, the more her tears fell. 'I'm not being ridiculous—it's true! I'm going to be ugly and tired and horrible, with long, lank hair and raccoon eyes, and nobody will *ever* want to have sex with me again!'

Bo pulled her forward so that she sat on the edge of the

bench and stepped between her knees. He cradled her face in his big hands and kissed the tip of her wet nose.

His voice was very soft and gentle when he spoke again. 'You are utterly gorgeous and...' through her tear-soaked eyes she saw his Adam's apple bob in his throat '...and men will flock to make love to you.'

'I'll have *twins*!' Remy howled. 'I'll be constantly exhausted and stressed and I will probably end up being an abusive mother!'

Bo tucked her head into his neck and gently rocked her. 'You won't. You'll be a wonderful mother. And I'll always look after you, Remy.'

Tears dripped from her neck onto the collar of his shirt. 'You can't *say* that. I'm not your responsibility, your problem. I have to do it myself. They are *my* babies.'

'You are strong enough to do this, Remy,' Bo said as she lifted her head to look at him. His thumbs swiped at the wetness under her lower lashes. 'You can *do* this—I promise.'

Remy dropped her eyes, wishing it were true. But this was her life, not a fairy tale. Bo was not going to rescue her. She'd have to do that herself.

'And I can give you a *very* good indication of how sexy you are,' Bo added, still standing between her spread legs, his broad hands on her knees.

Remy looked up at him, rapidly blinking her eyes. 'What's that?'

'Look down, Remy.'

Remy dropped her eyes to look at his chest.

'No, further.'

Remy's tears dried up when she saw the long length of him tenting his pants. She stared at his crotch for a moment, before lifting her eyes back up to his.

'Yeah... I don't even need to touch you to get turned on. You might be pregnant, but you're still all woman, still

sexy, still someone I'd like to taste again, tease again…
someone whose breathy cries I want to hear as she falls
apart in my arms.'

Bo dropped to his haunches and his hands gripped her
knees.

'I remember your taste, your smell, how fabulous we
were together. And, trust me, I'd love to be in your bed
again, inside *you* again.'

Remy licked her lips and placed her hands on his thick
wrists, loving the feel of his skin, of the crisp fabric of his
turned-back cuffs brushing her skin. 'I want that too…'

'But?'

'Complicated. *So* complicated.'

Remy dropped her head and rested it on his collarbone.
She sighed when his hand came up to grasp the back of
her neck, holding her head in place. Warm, strong, safe.

'Promise me something?' he said.

'Yeah?'

'If you get the urge to have one last sexual fling before
you get big and bulky come to me, okay?'

Since he was the only contender, that was an easy
enough promise to make. 'If I decide to complicate our
lives further, it's a deal.'

Bo just held her head, and she felt his lips in her hair.
'Would it be so bad, Remy? You and I sleeping together?'

Remy turned her face so that she was facing the wall,
knowing she should pull away but not able to do so just
yet. 'I'm not relationship material, Bo. I have far too many
issues about marriage and control to be successful at one.'

'I don't want a relationship either.'

'So what were you thinking? Benefits with your baby
mama?'

'The hell if I know.' Bo shrugged. 'All I know is that
you frustrate the hell out of me, mentally and sexually,

and you're going to drive me insane.' He cradled the side of her face in his big hand. 'I want you—don't doubt that.'

'I want you too. But I'm a big believer in keeping things simple and prioritising what's important. Sex isn't. Building a relationship on friendship and respect because we're having children together is. Having sex will always complicate that—taint that.'

Remy looked up at the ceiling and let out a long stream of air.

'I don't want to con myself, Bo, but I'm also human. I don't want to sleep with you and get so caught up in the fantasy of having my hot lover's babies, starting to play happy families, to find that once the bloom and the excitement wears off we're only together because of a one-night stand that carried on way past its sell-by date. I don't want to be stuck in a situation that I can't get out of, that is messy. I don't *do* messy.'

Bo dropped his hand and stepped away. 'You don't pull any punches either.'

'But am I wrong?'

Bo rubbed the back of his neck in agitation. 'I suppose not. I'm not ever going to remarry, fall in love again, so maybe it is better to keep our distance…sexually.'

And didn't *that* statement feel like a hot poker rammed into her chest?

'Did you love her that much?'

Bo lifted his head and looked her in the eye, his eyes deep and dark. 'I *still* love her that much.'

There was absolutely nothing she could say in response to that.

CHAPTER SEVEN

AFTER SUPPER BO returned to his office in the administration block, and instead of working, as he'd intended to do, he sat on his desk and allowed himself to look back on the day, to remember standing in that dark room with Remy, watching the synchronised beating of his twins' hearts.

Standing up, he went to the credenza on the far wall, hauled out a bottle of whiskey and a glass and poured himself a healthy shot. In between sips he pulled his tie off, threw it onto the antique coffee table in the lounge area and walked over to the floor-to-ceiling windows to watch the moonlight glint off the vines, which were heavy with grapes.

Seeing those smudges on the monitor had moved him far more than he'd expected. Before that he'd accepted Remy's pregnancy on a cerebral level, but seeing the living proof of their twins had smacked him in his emotional solar plexus. He was thankful that the room had been darkened. It had effectively hidden his watery eyes. It had been the first time in five years that he'd felt any true, visceral emotion apart from grief...

He'd been intrigued, amazed, nervous and utterly overwhelmed. It had taken all his concentration and willpower to listen to Dr Graham, to hear what he had to say...to fight against the powerful urge to take Remy in his arms. He could have spent a very long time just holding Remy and watching those two heart beats flutter in the kidney shapes on that small monitor.

He'd felt happy, he realised. And excited, grateful— amongst other feelings that he'd been a stranger to for a long, long time.

Bo turned his back on the moonlight drenched vines and, as per normal, looked across the room to the portrait of Ana. He let his eyes drift over her features, reminding himself of the curve of her cheek, the slant of her eyes. Since Remy had catapulted back into his life he'd hardly had time to think about Ana. He didn't want her to fade from his mind, to be relegated to a dark and dusty corner. She was still his wife…

But he'd soon be the father of another woman's children and Ana was *dead. They should've been our kids, honey, I would've changed your mind eventually,* he told her silently. But for the first time he couldn't imagine Ana having his children. When he tried to put her onto that couch in that room with the sonar scan, Remy's face and body appeared.

I promised I'd love Ana for ever. I told Remy that I still loved her… That was the truth.

Wasn't it?

Bo tossed his whiskey back, felt the burn of the liquor in the back of his throat and rested the cool glass against his forehead. Everything had changed, he thought, feeling his throat tighten. Over the past few years the one constant he'd had, the only truth he'd held on to, was the fact that his hopes and dreams of having a family, of being a lover, a husband and father, had been died with Ana on the side of the road.

One night with Remy had crumbled the foundations of that belief.

He was going to be a father—that was cast in stone. He

also wanted to be a lover—Remy's lover—and had even suggested it to Remy earlier. Where did that leave Ana?

Dead, his inner voice of reason answered prosaically.

But he still loved Ana—still wished that she was here, still missed her. How could he still be grieving for her and yet wanting Remy with his next breath? How could he reconcile the two? It didn't make sense...the two emotions should be incompatible.

He loved his wife...he'd promised to love her for ever...

But Remy was here: gorgeous, sexy, trying so hard to tough her way through a difficult situation. She was braver than he'd thought and more vulnerable than she portrayed herself as being. She had hidden depths, and he knew that there was a lot more to her than her being a traveller-cum-cook. She fascinated him in ways that Ana never had...

Not fair, he chastised himself. Ana had been an open book and Remy was...not. He knew next to nothing about her.

Bo glanced at his computer and thought about doing an internet search on her. Or he could pick up the phone and ask his private investigator friend to do a background check on her. He should know who he was having children with—what her background was, what he was getting into.

Or, that annoying inner voice suggested, *you can just ask her. Besides, it isn't like you can ask her to send the twins back if you don't like what you find out...*

Bo ran his hand over his jaw and held his chin. The problem was that he already liked her a bit too much, and he didn't know if finding out anything negative about her would change that.

He wanted her. It was that easy and that difficult.

Bo walked over to the credenza and for the first time in five years picked up the photograph of his wife and placed it face down on the wooden surface. Feeling disloyal, he immediately picked it up again and put it back in its proper place.

His jaw firmed and his back straightened. Ana would stay exactly where she was…in his heart and in his thoughts. It would take more than a gorgeous, sexy, funny woman to dislodge her from his life—even if she *was* carrying his twins.

Bo looked up at the sharp rap on his door and saw his cousin leaning his shoulder into the door frame, his hands in the front pockets of a pair of dirty worn jeans. He was wearing a massive grin that had Bo straightening.

'We're ready to rock and roll?' he asked, his excitement over what that smile meant kicking his sombre mood into touch.

'Harvest time.' Eli nodded. 'The Pinot Noir is ready to harvest. Ready to get your hands dirty, pretty boy?'

Six weeks had passed on Belleaire. It was mid-October and the harvest was finally over, Remy thought, staring out of the kitchen window of Bo's house. All the varieties of grapes had been picked, starting with the delicate Pinot Noir and the Syrah, which had been hand-picked. The Cabernet Sauvignon had been the last variety to be harvested and now everyone—especially the three owners of Belleaire—could take a deep breath and congratulate themselves on a good haul.

Or they could if they slowed down for ten seconds to do that.

Remy took a sip of her tea and pulled a face at her reflection in the glass. Bo had been up at daybreak for weeks, and she knew that he'd spent time in the vineyards, harvesting grapes himself, before rushing back to his house to shower and change for meetings. Then he'd return to the fields to help Eli, and after the sun went down he'd either go back to his office to catch up on his work or hit the desk in his study down the passage.

In between planning the menus for the bistro and testing the recipes she'd done some consultancy work for a Silicon Valley tech company, which had paid well but bored her to tears. She'd also taken to making meals for Bo, Ginny and Eli… Breakfast wraps, club sandwiches for lunch, dinners that they could quickly reheat before falling, exhausted, into bed.

Remy couldn't believe that the weeks had passed so quickly. At thirteen weeks her stomach was slightly rounder, her breasts considerably bigger, and the babies were, for the most part, out of the woods. She'd picked up the weight she'd lost when she'd been so ill, but she still was thinner than she should be.

On the plus side, the debilitating tiredness and the nausea had gone. She felt…well, wonderful. Strong, and healthy, and very strangely sexy.

Sexy… Hmm, that was a tame word for horny as hell.

Remy saw some movement in the vineyards and sighed when she saw Bo and Eli walking down the row of vines. Blond and dark…tall and built and so, *so* hot. If Bo had been alone she doubted whether she'd have had the willpower to keep from walking to him and plastering her mouth to his, to keep from running her hands up and under that sweatshirt, from unbuttoning the snap of his jeans.

'Good-looking devils, aren't they?' Ginny asked from her seat at the table, a bottle of beer on the table in front of her.

God, she'd kill for a glass of wine, thought Remy.

'Mmm…' she replied, trying to sound as non-committal as possible.

Ginny didn't need to know that many times over the past weeks she'd contemplated having a quick affair with Bo, but each and every time had nixed the idea. On a purely sexual level, to have Bo and then be denied the pleasure of his lovemaking would be hell, and she'd be even more frustrated than she currently was. How would she cope with the additional memories in the years to come? Honestly, reliving one night of mind-blowing passion was hard enough; remembering a couple of *months* of passion would be the equivalent of Chinese water torture—not that she knew exactly what that was, but it sounded horrible.

She blew air from her cheeks. They'd agreed to keep things simple, she reminded herself. Sex equalled complicated.

'I've never seen Bo spark off someone as he does with you,' Ginny stated, pushing back her messy blonde hair. Like her partners, she'd been working non-stop and she looked exhausted.

Remy turned away from the window and looked at Bo's sister. 'Surely he and Ana…?'

Ginny tipped her head. 'Ana was… Ana—someone we grew up with. She had no secrets.'

'And I do?'

Ginny lifted her eyebrows. 'Honey, we still know next to nothing about you. '

'Nobody has asked,' Remy pointed out. Her past wasn't a secret, but neither did she go around announcing that she was MENSA member with mommy issues.

And, talking about mommies, maybe she should tell her own mother that she was going to be a grandmother and that her new baby was going to be an uncle. Oh, boy…

'Bad timing…the past few weeks have been crazy. Harvest always is.' Ginny took a sip of beer. 'So, what's going on between you and Bo?'

'We're having twins together.'

Ginny rolled her eyes at this statement of the obvious. 'I meant…romantically.'

Remy was quick to shake her head. 'Nothing.' She saw

the look of disbelief and hastened to reassure her. 'Really—nothing! I'm not good at relationships, I don't believe in happy-ever-after, and Bo had and lost his. So we're just going to try and be friends, so that we can be the best parents we can to these two.' Remy touched her stomach.

Ginny stared at her for a long moment. 'That is the biggest load of rubbish I've ever heard! You two are doing a wonderful job of conning each other *and* yourselves.'

Remy found it hard to keep eye contact. 'I'm not sure what you mean.'

Ginny snorted. 'You know exactly what I mean. There is *nothing* friendly between you. Hot, lusty passion, maybe— but friendship? You're dreaming if you believe that.'

'We're going to be in each other's lives for long time, Ginny. It's not clever to start something that will end badly.'

'Who says it has to end?'

'Now who's dreaming?' Remy scoffed. 'It always ends, Ginny—always. Usually when I mess it up…' She held up her hand. 'This isn't just about us, Ginny, we have two other people to consider as well.'

Ginny pushed her chair back as she stood up. Walking over to Remy, she placed her hands on Remy's shoulders and squeezed. 'Bo wants a family. He operates best in a secure relationship and he likes you. You look like you need a place to land, and you won't find a better man. And you want to rip each other's clothes off… Both of you should stop thinking for five minutes and start *feeling*.'

Uncomfortable with Ginny's intensity and, worse, with the longing Ginny's words made her felt, Remy thought that it was best to change the subject.

She folded her arms across her chest and caught Ginny's eye. 'So, how's *your* love life, Ginny?'

'Shocking!' Ginny replied cheerfully. 'I haven't had sex in for *ever* and am convinced that I'm going to die an old maid!'

'*Are* you?'

Ginny shrugged. 'I'm not opposed to the idea. I like being on my own… I enjoy my own company. I feel… *smothered*…when I'm in a relationship. I don't need to talk to someone, see someone every day. And I always seem to hook up with men who want the package: marriage, double beds, kids…being entangled day after day, night after night.' She shuddered dramatically. 'Ugh.'

'Yet you're happy to push Bo and I into that?' Remy said, her tone dry.

Ginny flashed her huge smile. 'Because *you* both have a picket fence tattooed on your butt.' Ginny leaned forward and kissed her cheek. 'I'm going to go home, take a shower and fall face down into bed—blissfully alone.'

Ginny looked at her expectantly, her head cocked.

Remy angled her head towards the fridge. 'Lasagne—your portion is on top.'

Ginny headed straight to the fridge. 'Even if you weren't incubating my nephews…'

What *was* it with the Tessiers and the idea that she was carrying boys? There was a fifty-fifty chance that there were girls in there too!

'…I'd keep you around just for your cooking skills.' Ginny told her as she sauntered out through the door. Poking her head back into the room, she waggled her eyebrows. 'I'm still convinced that you would be a fabulous sister-in-law.'

Remy picked up an apple from the fruit bowl on the table and threw it at her.

Ginny snatched it out of the air and took a bite, before ambling off, leaving her scent and her laughter behind.

A few nights later Bo and Remy stood on his porch, watching Ginny and Eli walking off to their respective houses. It was the first meal they'd all shared together since before the harvest had started and Remy had cooked, using the opportunity to run some of her ideas for the bistro past the three of them. They'd had pulled pork, scallops, yellowtail and Thai green curry. They were all full to bursting, but Bo had known from the first bite that they'd found their permanent chef/manager for the Blue View.

Bo rubbed the back of his neck. like their plans for Bella's Folly, the Blue View Bistro had been neglected these past weeks. Now that the grapes were in he could get stuck in and make some decisions, and he was more than happy to cross finding a chef for the bistro off his long list of things to do.

That was if Remy would consider taking the job… He had no idea what she was thinking from one moment to the next.

Bo slid his arm around Remy's waist and gave her a quick squeeze. He could feel the thickening of her waist, had long ago noticed her swelling breasts. She'd always been on the scrawny side, and the small amount of weight she'd picked up suited her. He'd never found her more sexy.

Bo moved his hand from her waist to between her shoulder blades and steered her inside. Immediately she started to clear up the debris from dinner. He stepped forward and, gripping her by the tops of her arms, shoved her onto the couch.

'Hey!'

'Hey, back at you. It's after midnight, you've spent most of the day cooking, you're exhausted and nobody but me and you is going to know that you didn't clear up tonight. And since it's my house, and I don't care, neither should you.'

'I can't go to bed and leave a mess. I'll never sleep.'

'Then *I'll* do it.'

Remy shook her head, and Bo felt his teeth grinding together as her eyes drooped closed. He felt like thumping his head against the nearest wall. *Why* wouldn't she let him look after her? He found it deeply ironic that for the last five years he'd had to fight off women wanting him to take care of them and the one he wanted to take care of wouldn't let him.

Screw irony—it sucked.

Bo held out his hand. 'Let's go to bed.'

That woke her up. Remy's eyes widened and he saw the panic in them. He took her hand, and before he could react she stepped closer to his chest. He felt her bump against his stomach, those fabulous breasts against his chest, and couldn't believe how turned on he was.

'Together?' Remy suggested, with far too much sex in her voice.

Bo closed his eyes and inhaled her perfume. For a brief moment he could believe that she wasn't pregnant, wasn't his responsibility. She was just a woman to whom he was absolutely, inexplicably attracted.

He lifted his hand and ran his thumb across her exposed collarbone. Her skin was luminous and creamy and she smelled of those mysterious scents that made a man's nose quiver. Lilies, powder, woman... He looked down at her chest, his eyes tracing the blue veins that ran along the tops of her breasts. He followed one with his finger, halting when he came to the barrier of her T-shirt. He heard her swift intake of breath, felt her hand clutching the fabric of his shirt. Glancing down, he noticed that she was gnawing her bottom lip, her eyes on the floor. Lifting her chin with his finger, he connected with her deep eyes and, like before, fell into temptation.

He finally slid his lips over hers, as he'd wanted to do for so many weeks. They were smooth and luscious. Her hands had flattened against his chest. He was as aware of her fingertips digging into his skin as he was of her softening mouth. She was more than he'd imagined—more intoxicating, more womanly, more exciting.

Simply *more*.

This was what he'd been waiting for. This kick of his heart…this buzz in his head. How had he lived so long without touching her? *Had* he lived?

Wrapping his hand tighter around her waist, he pulled her closer and, clasping her face in his hand, deepened the kiss, falling into her mouth. Surely he was allowed this momentary pleasure? This brief respite from constantly wanting her?

Needing to explore, Bo ran his hands down her back, over her hip and up the sides of her ribcage. He ignored Remy's soundless plea to touch her breasts…if he did he wouldn't be able to stop. He tasted her, savouring her for one last time, before reluctantly dropping his hands and running his hand over his face, around the back of his neck.

Remy sat down on the couch and placed her hand on her stomach. *Oh, that's right… There's the other reason why I can't screw her senseless…the twins.*

Remy read his mind. 'Dr Graham said that if we didn't swing from the chandeliers sex should be fine.'

Bo's mouth fell open. 'You've discussed this with him?'

'He *is* my ob-gyn.' Remy placed a hand on the cushion behind her and stretched. 'And he brought it up…as did Ginny earlier.'

She'd lost him. 'What?'

'Apparently we have something cooking, Bo—some hectic electricity that people are noticing. Are we going to carry on ignoring it? Or are we going to give in and do what we both want to do?'

'God, I really want to,' Bo admitted quietly, sitting down next to her and placing a hand on her slim thigh. 'I don't know how much longer I can resist you. The memories of that night ambush me all the time.'

Remy linked her fingers in his. 'Me too.' She closed her eyes. 'It'll end badly, and we might end up hating each other—where will that leave us?'

Bo's breath skimmed across her hair. 'I know, Rem. My body just doesn't want to listen to my head. And I have a feeling that this…this need for each other is stronger than our intellect.'

Remy pulled her feet up onto the couch and snuggled down, so that her head was lying on his strong thigh. 'That's never happened to me before…my intellect has always been up-front and centre.'

Bo pulled a strand of hair off her cheek and allowed his fingers to drift lightly across her jaw. 'What do you mean?'

'We really don't know that much about each other, do we?'

Remy sighed and rolled onto her back so that she was staring up at him. He placed his hand on her stomach, feeling the rounded proof of his children.

'Harvest time is always chaos, and there isn't much time for chatting,' Bo replied, trying to keep down his rising excitement at finally being allowed to peek under the surface. 'I'm here now, and listening. Talk.'

Remy thought for a moment. 'Well, I guess the first thing you should know about me is that I'm smart.'

'I know that.' This wasn't news, Bo thought, disappointed.

'You don't understand. I'm pretty much always the smartest person in the room.' There was no false pride in her voice—she sounded as if she was ordering a pizza. 'I have a PhD in computer science and I received it a couple of months after my twentieth birthday.'

Ok, that *was* smart. That was *stupid* smart. Bo tried to connect the dots. 'So how does a woman with a PhD in computer science end up travelling and picking up strange men in bars?'

'What? Aren't smart girls allowed to want sex?' Remy narrowed her amazing eyes at him.

'I'm all for women wanting sex—especially if they're beautiful and smart and want to have it with me.' Bo smiled at her, pushing away the thought of how often she'd picked up other guys in bars. *Not going there,* he told himself.

Not. Going. There.

Remy sat up, turned to face him, and sat cross-legged on the couch next to him. Her elbow was pushed into the side of her knee and her chin rested on her fist. 'I graduated and landed a job at Tiscot's in their IT department. I got rapidly promoted and four years later was appointed as their CIO.'

Bo made some swift calculations. 'You only held the position for a year?'

'And a bit. It was long enough to put me into hospital with a perforated ulcer.' Remy lifted a shoulder. 'I was pretty sick…and depressed and unhappy. So I gave it all up and walked away to travel.'

Easily said, Bo thought, but not easily done. 'That's a hell of a decision.'

Remy leaned back and folded her arms. 'I heard all the arguments about why I shouldn't from my mother—there's nothing you can say that I haven't heard before. I know that I'm wasting my brain, wasting opportunities, not reaching my potential. I *know*…okay?'

Bo wanted to tell her that she was pushing her own buttons, but checked the words at his teeth. Instead he gripped her foot in his hand and squeezed. 'Was it the right decision for you? Did leaving make you happier?'

Remy's eyes filled with confusion at his questions. 'Absolutely.'

'Then why would I judge that?' Bo asked her, keeping his tone mild. He waited for a minute before probing some more. 'I take it that your mother wasn't supportive?'

'My mother is only supportive when I'm marching to the beat of her drum—when I'm making her look good, doing what I should,' Remy stated bitterly. Frustrated, she ran a hand over her face. 'Ignore that… I'm just tired. My mother and I have…issues. She's very smart, very driven, very ambitious, and she hates the fact that I'm not achieving as she'd like me to.'

Remy fiddled with the silver beaded bracelet on her wrist.

'She's just had her second baby and I'm hoping that he's not…not so smart.'

'Whoa…back up! Your mother has just had a *baby*? But—'

Remy smiled. 'She's only forty-four. She had me when she was seventeen. Can you imagine being seventeen and raising a gifted child? I taught myself to read when I was three…'

Bo shook his head in disbelief. 'How does your mom feel about having grandchildren who will be less than a year younger than her own child?'

Remy couldn't meet his eyes. 'Ah…that… Well, I haven't told her yet.'

Ah, hell. 'Are you planning on telling her? Or are you going to spring it on her when you go into labour?'

'The idea has its merits…' Remy muttered. 'You don't understand, Bo, she'll go nuts. You have no idea how crazy my mother can be when she loses it. And she *will* lose it. This is not in her plan for me. She's still trying to persuade me to go back to the corporate world or return to academia—go back into researching and working on AI.'

'AI?'

'Artificial intelligence.' Remy waved her hand as if to dismiss the subject—as if developing artificial intelligence was *nothing*. 'I don't want to disappoint her again… She tends to…'

Bo lifted his eyebrows, waiting for her to finish.

'To withdraw, to hold back…to whip back her approval.'

And you're still looking for it—probably looking for her love too. Complicated girl, Bo thought. Very smart and very complicated.

So, nothing new about this situation, then.

'Are you going to ask her to support you? For money? For help with the twins?' Bo asked.

'No.'

'Then she doesn't have a right to pass comment on anything you do. You're an adult, Remy—possibly a bit too smart for your own good, but still an adult. Tell her you're pregnant, tell her to deal with it and move on.'

Remy looked at her hands. 'You make it sound so easy.'

'It *is* easy,' Bo replied, his hand stroking her thigh. 'What *isn't* easy is wanting you and having you in the room next door, knowing that you're off-limits. Is there any way around that?'

Bo held his breath as he waited for her answer. 'We should be talking about the future…about the twins, our situation. The danger period has passed and I should be thinking of moving out, finding my own place. I should be making plans for the future.'

He'd heard a lot of 'shoulds' in there, so just waited for her to continue.

'I'm thirteen weeks pregnant, Bo.'

What did *that* have to do with the price of eggs? 'Yeah… so…?'

'I'm thirteen weeks pregnant and I have maybe eleven or twelve weeks to go before I get very big and bulky and sex becomes…challenging. After I give birth I am going to be the mommy of twins, and doing it single-handed is going to exhaust me.'

'I told you I would help—'

Remy held up her hand to interrupt him. 'I appreciate

that, but you won't be able to get up at night and breast-feed them, Bo.'

Good point.

'Anyway, the point I'm trying to make is that it will be a while before I'll be in a position to have a love life and I enjoy sex—especially with someone who knows what he's doing.'

Bo's ego puffed out its chest.

'So maybe we can do it for the next little while, and then when I get too big we can stop and use that time to transition into being friends who are co-parenting.'

If only she'd give him a chance to show her how good he could really be… Wait—hold on…*what*? Had she just said *yes*?

Bo frowned. 'Run that by me again?'

Remy lifted one eyebrow. 'Would you like me to draw you a picture? Would that help?'

Bo swiftly turned, lifted his hand to cradle her face. His eyes laughed into hers. 'You are *such* a smart-ass.'

Remy nodded, her eyes on his mouth. 'The tests *did* tell me that.'

He grinned as he ducked his head to kiss her, intending to be soft and gentle. But as soon as his lips met hers all his good intentions flew out of the window. He'd been lusting after her for days, weeks, constantly entranced by her sparkling eyes and her sharp mind. At that moment he could no more have stopped himself from kissing her than he could stop the sun from shining.

She tasted of Thai food they'd eaten earlier, hot and spicy, and her mouth was warm as her lips opened to receive his probing tongue. In typical Remy fashion she held nothing back, her passion rising with his as their kisses became deeper and longer. With his help she twisted so that she was nestled in his lap. His erection swelled his jeans and probed her thigh. Her one hand fisted in his hair and her other hand rested inside the collar of his shirt, tracing circles on his skin.

Bo skimmed his hand up her side, over the thin long-sleeved T-shirt she wore. She tensed as he caressed her thickened waist, and through his kisses he murmured words of reassurance. She'd never been so beautiful, blossoming with life. Scooting his hand under her shirt, he caressed her stretched stomach, feeling the wonder of soft skin over her hard belly. Moving higher, he cupped her enlarged breast, instinctively seeking her nipple, which instantly bloomed in his hand—a sharp, spiky response to his thumb gliding across its nubby surface.

Remy gasped and wrenched her mouth away from his, arching her back as she buried her face in his neck and swiped her tongue across his skin. *This* was what he remembered: this intensity, this flood of lust and emotion that he hadn't experienced since.

Bo groaned as his hands met at her back and unsnapped her bra, pulling it away to let her breasts fall naturally into the cup of his hands. Laying her across his lap, resting her back on the arm of the couch, he drew her shirt over her head and took in the wonder of her bare torso. Her jeans were tucked under her tummy, beautifully rounded with pregnancy. Her nipples were darker than he remembered, but her breasts were just as firm and tasted just as sweet.

Somewhere in the distance he heard her moan, felt her fingers under his shirt as they danced across his belly. His concentration was fierce as he took his time, alternately sucking and licking her magnificent breasts. Even as she squirmed, silently arching her hips for more, he carried on, not quite done with his physical adoration.

Bo sensed Remy's frustration and responded with a silent chuckle. She wasn't the only one who craved more; his penis was as hard as stone and desperate to escape the confinement of his jeans. But this wasn't about him.

Tonight was about Remy and the pleasure he could give her—better and bolder than the pleasure she'd experienced when he'd last held her naked in his arms.

'Lift your hips, sweetheart,' he murmured against her mouth, and Remy, eyes glazed with passion, obliged.

Bo pulled down her jeans with one hand, his eyes locked on her face as he fumbled with her shoes, eventually tossing the annoying articles to the floor. Her jeans followed and she lay across him, her femininity hidden by a tiny triangle of soft rose cotton. Her thighs were slim and baby-smooth; he could feel her hip bone next to the place where her stomach ballooned.

Bo kissed her shoulder as he whispered, 'You're so incredibly beautiful.'

Remy hiccupped her laugh. 'Beautifully *fat*.'

'Beautifully gorgeous,' Bo insisted, before capturing her mouth again and only breaking the kiss to help her pull his shirt over his head.

Then her hands were all over his chest, his shoulders, sneaking towards his belt buckle. She managed to undo his belt, unsnap his jeans button, but before he lost control he held her wrists together with one hand.

'Let me pleasure you?' Bo asked, and saw the soft reply in her eyes, tasted it in her lifted lips.

She became compliant beneath him, her trust that he would take care of her blindingly obvious.

While kissing her—he couldn't get enough of her luscious mouth—Bo moved his hands to her slender ankles, tracing his way up her calves to her thighs, lingering to knead her bottom. His long fingers slid under her bottom, probing to stroke lightly between her legs. Unconsciously, Remy let her thighs fall open, and Bo could see the sudden dampness of her panties.

He ignored Remy's whimper as he removed his fingers, felt her subsequent intake of breath as he trailed his hand over her pubic mound, bending his head to suck her breasts as he drew circles across the fabric, feeling her soft curls beneath his fingertips. Needing to feel her, he ripped the fabric away, and neither of them noticed nor cared that the flimsy fabric ripped at her hips, allowing him quicker access to her warm, secret places.

His fingers—urgent now—slid over and into her furrows, automatically finding her clitoris, causing her to lift her hips, thrusting into his hand. Astounded at her passionate reaction, by the tension he could feel in her, Bo felt immensely powerful, intensely male. At that moment he absolutely believed that he had been put on this earth to give Remy pleasure, and he proceeded to do exactly that.

Fingers probed and entered her, his thumbs caressing that centre of pleasure until she was whimpering into his neck, begging for release. When he felt that she was close he removed his fingers and, ignoring her protestations and his own demand for sexual release, slowed the process down by kissing her mouth, and her breasts, before taking his mouth south and kissing her intimately—until she crested and flew, before sinking back to earth murmuring his name.

Pulling him up, Remy cradled his head into her neck, half sobbing from the pleasure of the experience. Bo felt her yawn and smiled as he tried to move, with Remy clinging like a limpet to his neck. Scooping her up, he held her close against his chest as he walked to her bedroom, pulling back the covers with one hand before placing her on the clean fresh sheets.

Kissing her lightly on the lips, he smoothed a hand over her tumbled hair as her hands dropped to her sides. 'Where are you going?' she asked sleepily.

'Bathroom. Be right back,' he replied.

'Mmm…okay.'

Bo stepped away from the bed and stood in the doorway that led to the en-suite bathroom. Remy yawned again, tucked her hands under her head and fell asleep. As he had known she would.

When he was sure she was fast asleep Bo moved from his position, pulled the bedcovers over her and kissed her forehead. 'Sweet dreams, Rem.'

And it was back to the shower for him…

CHAPTER EIGHT

REMY BOLTED UPRIGHT, saw that she was in her own bed and that it was empty. She slapped her hand against her mouth. She'd happily taken the orgasm Bo had given her and promptly passed out. He must think she was the biggest tease in creation...

On the plus side, it had been the best sleep she'd had in ages...

Remy shoved her hands into her hair and pushed it away from her face. How should she handle this? Handle him? Should she joke her way through it? Apologise? Beg him to come back to bed so that they could do it properly? She'd propositioned him once before—why was it so difficult to do it now?

The last time it had been about sex with a stranger... Bo wasn't a stranger any more. She knew him. Not well, admittedly, but better than she had before. She knew that he worked like a demon, hated peanut butter, and that he drank beer when he was relaxed and Irish whiskey when he was stressed.

She knew that he wanted her—but not enough to take her to his bed, to show her the room he'd shared with his wife. It hadn't escaped her notice that Bo had brought her back to *her* room; she instinctively knew that if they were about to embark on a sexual affair, then it would be in this room. His room was, and would always be, off-limits.

His wife still occupied that space…

Aaargh! She had no right to be even vaguely perturbed, even a smidgeon upset by that thought. She and Bo had agreed to an affair, to sex, and where they did it shouldn't worry her. She was *not* going to get emotionally attached—she couldn't and wouldn't.

This was sex—pure and simple. Sex with a little liking thrown in, but nothing more.

You're starting off on a very bad foot, Draycott, she warned herself. *Pull yourself together immediately!*

'Was it that bad?'

Remy jumped at Bo's voice and snapped her head up, her mouth and eyes softening as they landed on him. He stood in the doorway to the bedroom, his hands gripping the door frame above him head, dressed only in a pair on unsnapped jeans. The muscles in his chest moved and his stomach muscles rippled. With his mussed hair and stubble he looked a little wicked and a lot disreputable. Hot. Sexy. Dangerous. How could she resist?

'I fell asleep.' She licked her lips as her eyes travelled down, and up over his body again.

'I noticed,' Bo replied dryly.

Remy, deciding that faint heart never won fair man, pulled off her shirt and leaned back against the pillows, fighting the urge to cover up her naked body. Bo's eyes glazed and his grip tightened as he examined her body, his eyes eventually landing on her rounded stomach. He stalked over to her, sat on the bed beside her. His hand was both hesitant and warm as he touched her bump.

'It's so beautiful. *You're* so beautiful.'

'Ever done it with a pregnant woman before?' Remy teased.

'Uh…no.'

'Well, I've never been pregnant before—so we're both virgins, in a strange way.' Remy placed her hand on the hot skin of his hip and slid it down so that she was gripping his hip bone under his loose jeans. 'I'll be gentle with you.'

'I appreciate your consideration…' Bo murmured as his dropped his mouth to hers.

They had much to discuss, Bo thought as he handed Ginny a cup of coffee. They were waiting for Eli to arrive at the first post-harvest meeting they'd managed to schedule and, frankly, it was a miracle that he'd managed to make it there at all.

Leaving a naked Remy, sleepy and sexy, had been a task of Herculean proportions.

Their one-night stand hadn't been a fluke. After they'd been sleeping together for a week, the sex kept getting better and better. She was a creative lover and she seemed to be as into him—sexually—as he was into her.

Two or three months, he reminded himself. That was all they had before she got too big and uncomfortable—before they had to make the transition to being friends and about-to-be co-parents.

He intended to make every moment count.

'Have you spoken to Remy about managing the bistro?' Ginny asked him, yanking him out of the bedroom.

'Uh…no, not really. Nothing formal has been decided,' Bo replied, pouring himself a cup of coffee and swallowing his yawn. If he was tired from being up all night, then Remy would be exhausted. He'd turned to her time and time again.

How much sex was too much? Was there a limit?

'Maybe we *should* formalise that.' Ginny frowned. 'I don't like the idea of her working for nothing.'

'I don't either, but she's so damn independent.' Bo sat on the edge of his desk and stretched out his legs. 'You two seem to have hit it off.'

Ginny tipped her head. 'I like her. She's smart. But

there's something about her that makes me want to protect her...'

'That's because you are a mother hen,' Bo teased. If Ginny could, she'd shoo everyone under her wing to keep them from bumping their heads or their hearts.

Ginny didn't bother arguing. 'So, has Ginny found somewhere else to live?'

Bo lowered his coffee mug to look at his sister. 'She's living with me.'

'But she doesn't want to stay there for ever. She's approached a couple of real estate agents, looking for a small cottage to rent.'

But now that they were sleeping together why would she want to move out? What the hell was happening?

He waved his mug in the air and the coffee threatened to spill over the sides. 'She's not earning a salary from us—how can she afford the rent?'

Ginny stood up and took the mug from his hands, placing it on the desk behind him. 'Honey, haven't you realised yet that the last thing Remy needs from you is money? Don't you two talk at *all*?'

Not much, no.

'According to one of my friends, who is an estate agent, Remy has has decided that she can't live with you—that she needs her own place...a place to bring her babies to that's a home. *Her* home.'

Bo couldn't identify the emotions boiling in his gut. Frustration, hurt, panic... 'My place can be her home.'

Ginny sighed in sympathy. 'No, darling, it can't. It was Ana's home. And, as welcome as you make her feel...' Ginny's face suggested that she knew they were sharing sheet time '...it's not a place where she can nest.'

'What does *that* mean?' Bo demanded, aggravated.

'Remy will want a nursery she can decorate. She needs

a place where she can put up photographs—paint the walls bright pink if that's what she wants to do.'

Bo blew out his breath and silently counted to ten. And then to twenty. 'I don't like the idea of her being on her own.'

'Me neither. I'd let her move in with me, but I don't think I want my walls painted pink.'

'*And* you like your space too much.'

Ginny folded her arms beneath her breasts, clutching at the fabric of her pink top. 'I do have an idea for what to do about Remy.'

Bo was happy to listen. His sister, as he'd discovered a lifetime ago, wasn't a fool.

Ginny stepped back and resumed her seat. 'Why don't you let her stay in the guest house? It's empty more often than not and it's just sitting there.'

He would—except for one little problem...he didn't want her to leave *his* house. His bed. The bed in the guest room, he clarified.

Ginny continued, swept away by enthusiasm, 'And Remy could pay you rent—which would make her happy.'

'But it doesn't make *me* happy,' Bo grumbled, walking around the desk and sinking into his chair.

'You know it's a good solution, Bo. She'll be close by if there's a problem, and once the twins are born you'll have easy access to them.' Ginny linked her hands around her knee. 'She needs to keep her independence, Bo—some pride. Let her find her feet, some solid ground. She needs that more than she needs you swooping in and dictating how her life should be.'

'Remy wouldn't listen to me anyway.'

Ginny smiled. 'Another reason I like her: she's won't roll over and let you scratch her tummy like—'

Ginny quickly looked away, but Bo knew what she had been about to say. *Like Ana did.*

'Ana was a totally different personality. She didn't *need* to make everything into a battle,' Bo muttered. Actually, before they married they never fought about anything and afterwards they stopped talking unless it was to argue about having kids. Their motorbike ride the morning of her death had been an attempt to reconnect, to rediscover the magic.

'Ana never argued about *anything*. Her favourite words were, "Yes, Bo."' Ginny lifted up her hand to stop the discussion. 'I loved Ana—you know that—but Remy…? Well, I love her too. Better than that, I *like* her. A lot.'

Ginny and Ana had been friends…sort of, Bo conceded. But she and Remy were already *close* friends—something she'd never managed to be with Ana. Should that mean something? And if it did, what?

He'd forgotten how damn complicated women could be.

'Sorry I'm late,' Eli said, walking into the office and tossing his ball cap onto the coffee table. 'Coffee—I need coffee.'

Eli poured himself a cup, sat on the edge of the couch and sipped. After a minute the caffeine hit his bloodstream and he looked up, his eyes bright and bold. 'I have news.'

'Good, I hope?' Bo replied, looking at the pile of folders on his desk.

'Do you remember I contacted that genealogy expert to find out who Bella's nearest heir was?' Eli asked as he placed his ankle on his knee.

Bo winced. That was another thing he'd meant to do but had forgotten while he'd been dealing with Hurricane Remy. 'I dropped that ball,' he admitted ruefully. 'Thanks for picking it up.'

Eli waved his gratitude away. 'Hearing that you're about to have twins with a one-night stand you're still lusting after would confuse any guy.'

Bo glared at him. 'Don't go there. What's the news?'

'Well, the genealogy tracers found somebody who will inherit.' Eli looked smug.

Ginny leaned forward. 'Who is the heir? And when can we contact him?'

'Well, turns out it's none other than the bad boy of rock Digby West! Who, according to his agent, has no interest in doing anything productive with the land other than making as much money from it as possible. '

'Wow! Okay, I didn't see that one coming!' quipped Bo. 'Does that mean he's receptive to an offer?' he demanded.

Eli shrugged and grinned again. 'According to his manager, he is.'

'Seriously?' Bo said, his excitement rising.

'Getting the genealogist involved was a genius move and one which no other interested party had thought of. Thanks to Remy's suggestion it meant I was first in line to get in touch with Mr West's business manager to make an offer. So there is a solid chance that Bella's Folly will soon be ours!'

Bo leaned back in his chair and twisted his lips. 'Eli— you are a legend!'

Ginny dropped her head into her hands and laughed loudly. 'Only *Bella's* closest heir would be a spoilt, materialistic, entitled pig of a celebrity. Lucky for us he's only interested in the money!

Bo nodded his agreement. Only Bella.

It turned out that hearing she was going to become a grandmother, and that her new son was to be an uncle before her first birthday, did not thrill her mother.

What a surprise, Remy thought.

She'd elected to tell her mother and grandmother face-to-face—she felt that she owed them that—so she made the long trip to Portland and their reactions—horrified—Jan—and surprised—Rosie—were what she'd expected.

What she hadn't expect was her mother resting her head into the crook of her arms and sobbing over her sleek kitchen table. Her mother never cried—*never*. Remy sent her grandmother a *Has she lost it?* look, and Rosie responded by lifting her shoulders in a helpless shrug.

'Mom? Is it such a tragedy that I'm pregnant?'

Jan lifted her tear-stained face and shook her head, obviously and utterly miserable. '*Anyone* can have babies,' she stated fiercely, 'but that mind—*your mind*—comes along once in a generation. And what are you doing with it? Nothing! Playing with menus and setting up a restaurant. You could be changing the world.'

'I don't want to change the world,' Remy protested.

'It doesn't matter what you want—it's your responsibility!' Jan stated, her skin blotchy with temper.

'I have a responsibility to these children too, and to myself,' Remy replied. 'I'm sorry that my choosing a…a gentler way of life and stepping away from the IT world upsets you so much, but I don't want what you want for me. I want a family. I want these children. I want to be… normal.'

'The problem is that you are *not* normal.'

Jan spat the words out and Remy recoiled; her mother's words were the emotional equivalent of hard steel stars striking her heart. She wasn't normal…but *damn* she wanted to be.

Rosie, ever the peacemaker between the two of them, stepped into the conversation. 'Tell us about the father.'

Glad to step off the subject of her normality—or lack thereof—Remy briefly explained that Bo was widowed and how excited he was about the children, how much he wanted a family.

'So you're basically his brood mare?' Jan commented, her eyes miserable.

'Are you *Hank's* brood mare?' Remy asked, irritated

with her negativity. Before her mother could answer Remy turned to Rosie and continued. 'We're going to co-parent these children—raise them together. Separate houses, separate lives, but sharing the twins.'

'You have *got* to be kidding me,' Jan muttered, leaning back and folding her arms. 'Does that mean that you're staying in Belle…whatever that town is called?'

'Bellevue,' Remy corrected her, and nodded reluctantly.

She'd never made a conscious decision to stay, but she knew that it was the logical, sensible choice. If she wanted her children to have a dad—and who wouldn't?—this was the way it had to happen. And Bellevue was an arty, sophisticated, vibey town—she'd liked the place from the moment she landed there.

And Bellevue held Belleaire, and Belleaire held Bo— who was becoming far more important to her than she'd ever imagined. And not only as the father of her babies.

Remy traced her thumbnail across the seam of the tablecloth and nibbled on her bottom lip. She couldn't imagine a life without Bo in it, and she was already dreading the moment when she would have to step back and away— when they'd change their status from temporary lovers to co-parents.

God, it was going to be horrible!

'Tell me about him,' Rosie demanded, running her spotted hand over Remy's head as she passed her on the way to the coffee pot.

Remy thought she'd keep it simple. 'He's successful, good-looking and smart.' She couldn't help the sour look she sent Jan. 'He's big into his family and has a protective streak a mile wide.'

Jan's eyes narrowed. 'Ah…*now* I get it.'

What crazy rabbit had her mother pulled out of her hat now? 'Get what?'

'Why you're doing this—why you're staying in that small town, attempting this co-parenting lark.'

'You and Hank are co-parenting—you're raising a child together. I don't understand your logic…you're acting crazy.' Remy shoved her hands into her hair and pulled. By the end of her visit she was convinced that she'd be pool-ball-bald.

'You just want a man to protect you and to support you—you've always wanted that. As a little girl you always asked for a daddy for Christmases and birthdays— that was your constant request.'

'Isn't that normal?' Remy demanded. Of course she'd wanted a father—preferably one who'd provide a balance to her mother's constant demands to work harder, be smarter, achieve more. Someone who'd love her for just being Remy.

'You should be *above* wanting what is normal! You're too smart for that!'

Remy's mouth dropped open and Rosie gasped her dismay.

'Mom, I am *not* a freaking robot! I am a human being with feelings and emotions and wants and needs. Just because I'm smart it doesn't mean that I don't deserve a family, or children, or a man standing in my corner.'

'When you receive such a blessing as your intellect you should be grateful and concentrate on that.'

Remy stared her down. 'Are you nuts? Where is this coming from?'

Jan stood up and placed her hands on the table, her eyes wild. 'You had everything, Remy! *Everything!* You could've had the world at your feet, money in the bank, accolades and recognition. You could've been *somebody*!'

This wasn't about her, Remy suddenly realised as understanding swept through her. This had nothing to do with her and everything to do with her mother's lost hopes and dreams. This was about the seventeen-year-old girl who'd fallen pregnant, who'd had to give up her scholarship to raise a child, who'd had to get her degree the hard way. This was about the young, brilliant scholar who'd felt hampered and hindered by her child, and about the mother who was still vicariously living through her daughter.

'Now you're going to be some man's convenience—this man's means of providing the family he so desperately wants! You've always complained about people—*me*—loving you, wanting you for the things you do and not for who you are. I find it so damn ironic that you're doing the same thing with this man.' Jan wiped her eyes with the tips of her fingers.

'That's *enough*, Jan!' Rosie snapped, placing her hand on Remy's shaking shoulder. 'That's more than enough!'

Jan looked up at her mother with wet, anxious eyes. 'She's wasting her life...wasting her brain. Wasting...*everything*.'

'That's your perception. And even if I agreed with you—and I don't—I would still say that it's her life to waste,' Rosie stated, her tone brooking no disagreement.

Remy, deciding that she'd had more than enough, pushed her chair back and quickly stood up. 'I'm sorry you feel this way, Mom, and I hope that someday we'll be able to move beyond this conversation and get to a place where you can think that I'm enough just because I'm Remy.'

She looked across the room to where Callum was asleep in his pram.

'All I ask of you is to not put the same crazy pressure on him that you did on me—no matter how smart he is. Tell him that he's worthwhile, that he's a blessing just because he's standing on this earth and breathing. That he doesn't need to be or do anything to feel worthwhile—that he's enough just as he is.'

Remy picked up her bag, slung it over her shoulder

and walked to the back door. Rosie followed her out and at her truck placed her hand against the side of her cheek. 'I think *you* are wonderful,' she said softly, 'just because you're standing here and breathing.'

Remy held her grandmother's hand against her face, relishing the familiarity of her touch, the comfort it always gave. 'I know you do.'

Rosie sent her a sad smile. 'For all your fancy words and your protestations, I just wish you believed it too.'

On the stage, bright-eyed couples stood around self-consciously, some of the women exchanging small talk while the men looked at the floor, the ceiling, or out of the window. Bo realised why they weren't making eye contact with the midwife, or each other, when he and Remy reached the group. On the free-standing board she'd pinned pictures of a sweating, screaming woman giving birth, her face contorted and her legs wide open.

Bo felt his stomach lurch. How quickly could he reach the door? Ten seconds? Twenty?

Earlier he'd been convinced that it was vitally important that he accompany Remy to antenatal classes. Suddenly he wasn't nearly so convinced.

He heard Remy's introduce him to the midwife, and when she pinched his side he wrenched his eyes from the board and focused them on a petite brunette with a wide smile and sparkling brown eyes. She barely seemed old enough to have sex, let alone lecture on childbirth.

After shaking his hand, Tarryn rapped her fist on the tabletop and the eager parents-to-be dropped into their chairs and gave her their full attention. Bo guided Remy to the last available chairs—smack in the middle of the front row and directly in front of the gruesome photos.

Tarryn started to speak, but Bo couldn't concentrate on a damn thing. Not when he was being constantly slapped in the face by the sight of the screaming woman trying to force a watermelon-sized baby through a hole made for a pea.

Bo lifted his hand, and when Tarryn acknowledged him he spoke. 'I'm sorry, but if I'm going to be here for the next ninety minutes can you turn that board around?'

Tarryn frowned, slightly confused, before following his pointed finger. Seeing the board, she laughed. 'Oh, good grief! I'd forgotten that was up. I use it as a deterrent when I talk to teenagers about safe sex.'

'Guess we're all past that,' Bo said dryly.

Tarryn rolled the board around and Bo relaxed when he saw serene pictures of rolling landscapes and calm seas. Right, he was now ready to be bored out of his skull. He'd read some baby magazines, and a couple of books, and felt he knew enough about pregnancy and childbirth to get through the process. He was here to support Remy. While the group discussed childbirth options and pregnancy symptoms he'd work through a couple of issues that were currently plaguing him.

He needed to think about his scheduled trip to the UK and France—he wasn't leaving Remy on her own so Eli would have to go in his place—and he wanted to work on the plans relating to how best to use Bella's Folly when Digby West finally got around to signing the papers. And then there was Remy, whom he was never *not* thinking about.

She'd been quiet since she returned from Portland two days ago, and Bo felt bad that he hadn't had time to ask how her mother and grandmother had taken the news about the pregnancy. She was growing bigger, Bo realised, eyeing her stomach. Their hectic, adventurous, utterly amazing sex-life was soon going to come to an end… Not even he would risk hurting the twins.

'Today we're going to talk about sex!' Tarryn chirruped.

Oh, my God, please don't, Bo muttered silently, and squirmed in his chair along with the rest of his sex. He'd spent far too much time thinking about sex and imagining what he intended to do to Remy that he had no desire to talk about it.

Besides, how could he listen to Tarryn lecture about sex when she looked as if she'd lost her virginity last week?

'So let's get this straight: you can make love even when you feel as big as a house and as sexy as a limp washcloth. But we *do* need to talk about positions—because I don't recommend the missionary position from about sixteen weeks' gestation,' Tarryn continued, either ignoring or blithely unaware of the flushed male faces.

Well, huh... On the plus side, maybe he and Remy could extend their agreement. But on the negative side they were talking about *sex*...with *pregnant women.* Discussing it went against every law of nature, and Bo felt as if he should hand in his man card. Why couldn't Tarryn just talk to the women about this and then they could pass the information along?

Bo forced himself to slouch in his chair, to paste a look of boredom on his face, but his eyes kept darting towards the open door. Tarryn stood up and lifted a pack of papers from the desk and Bo groaned internally as he caught a glimpse of the illustrations. The *Kama Sutra* for pregnant couples? God, please shoot him now.

He could feel Remy's shoulder shaking against his and risked a glance at her face. She had her bottom lip firmly between her teeth and she was staring intently at the floor, fighting laughter.

'This is *so* not funny!' Bo hissed in her ear.

Remy gurgled. 'You insisted on coming with me.'

Bo glared at her as he accepted a set of Tarryn's papers, carefully placing it face down on his knees.

Bo squirmed through descriptions of 'woman on top',

spooning, hands and knees, and side-lying. He heard about shallow penetrations and stimulating the clitoris and the need to be creative…

Tarryn took a sip of water and Bo silently begged her to shut up. He wasn't sure how much more he could take. Listening to her was like watching a particularly steamy sex scene at the movies. Enough to titillate but stopping just short of tipping into porn. Either way, he was horribly uncomfortable.

'Okay, so let's talk about orgasms,' Tarryn suggested.

Did she expect them to answer? Bo wanted to put up his hand and say that he'd like another one in the very near future, if that could be arranged, just to see her reaction.

'So, orgasms can be different during pregnancy—and some woman only orgasm during pregnancy when they never could before.'

'Not something *you* suffer from,' Bo muttered, his head tipped towards Remy.

Remy shoved her elbow into his ribs. 'Shut up!'

Bo heard a low groan from the back of the room, and he sympathised. He'd give up his credit line to be anywhere else but here…preferably in a bed with Remy.

'So, orgasms are really good for you *and* your baby. The baby experiences the same euphoric hormone rush that you do—'

So, hell, even the twins got in on the action? That sounded a bit creepy…

'Now, let's go on to sex after birth,' Tarryn suggested—as if they actually had an option. Which they didn't. 'Many women aren't very interested in sex for at least three months after the birth and some take a lot longer. You might battle, Remy, being run off your feet with two babies to look after.'

'I'll hire you an army of nurses if it means you'll find your libido faster,' Bo suggested, *sotto voce*. The couples on either side of them picked up his muted words and laughed. Remy aimed another elbow into his ribs.

'We won't be having sex then, remember? We'll just be friends.'

Oh, right. Damn.

Tarryn grinned. 'I see a couple of men ready to bolt, so we'll change the subject. But before I forget you'll need to bring a mat to next week's class,' Tarryn told them.

Bo's eyes widened. His heart sank to his toes. *What the hell for?*

He decided he'd just rather not know.

CHAPTER NINE

REMY WAS WALKING past Bo's bedroom when she saw movement behind his partially open door. Stopping, she stuck her foot out and—whoops, look at that!—the door opened. Leaning her shoulder into the door frame, she watched Bo pull on his trainers, then snap the band to his heart-rate monitor around his broad chest, completely unaware that she was watching him. Beautiful man, she thought, as she always did.

His room... Ana's room... Up until this point she'd absolutely and resolutely respected his wish to keep her out and, as hard as it had been to keep her curiosity in check, she'd never once opened this door. Not even to take a quick peek.

Thinking that he had a right to know that she was there, she cleared her throat and he looked up, his eyes wary. When he didn't shoo her away Remy took half a step across the threshold and stood next to the tall credenza at the entrance of the room.

It was lovely, Remy admitted, looking around in frank curiosity. The walls were a pale shade of aqua, except for the one behind the huge leather headboard, which had been painted a deep rich brown, and pen and ink sketches of his family, of Belleaire, Bellevue and the surrounding areas, were grouped on the walls.

There were no photographs except for the massive

portrait above his bed. It could only be Ana, gorgeously mussed, sleepy and sexy, and obviously naked beneath the sheer sheet that was draped over her curvaceous body.

Okay, so that explained why he'd never feel comfortable sleeping with her in his own bed. There was no way they could share such uninhibited, joyful, stupendous sex with her looking down at them.

Bo saw her looking at the portrait and the steel shutters in his eyes dropped. Remy shook her head and held up her hand. 'Don't do that,' she chided softly.

'Do what?' Bo challenged.

'Retreat…close yourself off.' Remy gestured to the photograph. 'She was your wife; you obviously loved her—'

Remy saw Bo's jaw tighten. 'I don't talk about Ana. Ever.'

'Why not? Doesn't she deserve to be spoken about?' Remy asked gently. 'Doesn't she deserve to be remembered?'

'Of course she does,' Bo said through gritted teeth.

'I understand why you won't discuss her with just anyone, but what I *don't* understand is why you won't discuss her *at all*. Not even with Ginny and Eli. If she deserves to be remembered, why don't you talk about her?' Remy asked, walking across the room to sit on the corner of his king-sized bed.

This was a conversation that they needed to have, she realised—that *he* needed to have.

Bo fiddled with his heart-rate monitor and ignored her question. Since he'd yet to kick her out of his room, or tell her to be quiet, she thought she'd push a little more. 'Is it because it hurts too damn much?'

She saw the answer in his quick shrug, in his bleak eyes. Yeah, it still hurt like crazy. Remy sent an envious glance up to the blue-eyed blonde. *Lucky girl,* she told her silently, *being loved by this utterly spectacular man.*

'Tell me something about her.'

Bo stared at the carpet between his feet and shook his head.

'It doesn't have to be something big,' Remy told him. 'Tell me something you remember…something funny…'

'Why?' Bo croaked. 'What's the point?'

The point is that nearly five years is far too long to keep all this emotion bottled up inside you.

'One thing, Bo,' Remy whispered, hoping that he'd take that tiny step. He needed to offload on someone, and besides, she was very curious about what it was about her that made Bo love her so intensely.

Bo took so long to speak that she didn't think that he'd engage with her, and Remy was surprised when he actually did.

He gestured to the photograph. 'She looks so relaxed, so sexy in that photograph, but she was actually seriously tipsy. It was the only way I could get her to take her clothes off—to pose like that.'

'*You* took that photograph?' Remy lifted her eyebrows, astounded. 'The colours and contrast are amazing—and so artistic. I thought it must have been done by a professional.'

Bo shook his head. 'Everyone thought that she was this hippy, free-spirited woman but that was the front she showed the world. Actually, she was pretty insecure and quite a prude. I had to get her half-wasted before she lost her inhibitions and allowed me to shoot her. I took that photo about a year before she died.'

'It's stunning.' Remy dropped her hand and stretched out on the comforter, resting her head in her hand. 'Who did the sketches?'

'Me again. In the early days, when I had more time, we used to pack a picnic basket and she'd take her book and I'd take my sketch pad and we'd spend the day outdoors.'

'Do you still miss her?'

Bo ran a hand through his hair. 'I did... I *do*. Not as much as I did,' he added reluctantly.

Remy bit the corner of her mouth and wondered whether she was brave enough to ask the question she most wanted the answer to. Gathering her courage, she traced the diamond stitching in the comforter with her fingernail.

'You obviously loved her very much, and everyone says that you had a brilliant relationship, so knowing that—having had that—why wouldn't you want to try and find it again? With someone else?'

Bo didn't hesitate to reply. 'Because I don't know if I can love someone else as much as I did her—and how do I enter a relationship knowing that? Knowing that Ana will always have the bigger piece of my heart? It won't be the same as what I had with Ana and I'll feel cheated. Worse, I'll cheat the woman I enter that relationship *with*.'

'Does it have to be the same?' Remy asked, her heart pounding in her chest. 'Why can't it be as good but different?'

Bo shook his head. 'I really don't think that's possible. Besides, I made a promise to Ana that I have to keep.'

'What promise?' Remy asked, knowing that he probably wouldn't tell her.

'I promised to love her.' Bo's words were tinged with desperation.

Okay...that wasn't a surprise. She knew that love didn't die with death—that it lived on regardless.

'You can love her and still have a relationship with someone else, Bo,' Remy replied. Why did he think that one excluded the other? Where did such a rigid idea of love come from?

'With who, Remy? *You?*' Bo slapped his hands on his hips and his face tightened. 'What are you getting at?'

'I'm just trying to understand you.'

Those eyes darkened, hardened, as he mentally retreated. 'You don't *need* to understand me. We're only sleeping together, and soon we'll stop doing that so there's no point. We're friends having a few months of sex—that was the deal, remember?'

She hadn't forgotten what they were doing—not for one second—but his words still stung like icy bullets. 'Jeez, calm down, Bo. It was just a random conversation.'

Bo's expression turned sarcastic. 'Sure it was.'

'Excuse me?'

'There's always a subtext to these conversations. I've had enough of them over the past five years,' Bo said, his expression grim.

Okay, now he was making her mad. 'Are you suggesting that I'm trying to figure out whether or not I have a chance with you?'

His indolent shrug and lifted eyebrow screamed, *Aren't you?*

'I am *not* advocating for a continuation of this relationship and I am *certainly* not pushing for more!' Remy shot to her feet, her eyes blazing.

'Then what was the point of talking about my dead wife?'

God save me from moronic males, Remy thought. 'I had a crazy thought that we were friends and that friends discuss things. It just goes to show how stupid I can be on occasion.'

Remy flounced over to the open door, but before she could leave his room Bo's hand on her elbow had her spinning around and she thumped into his chest. As per usual, her blood started to hum and her skin prickled. She could be dead and he would still turn her on, Remy admitted reluctantly. It was supremely annoying.

'This is why I don't like talking about Ana.' Bo said his eyes hot and frustrated. 'It always leads to an argument.'

Remy jerked her arm out of his grip. 'No, it leads to an

argument because you're an idiot. I just wanted to know a little about your past. I might not be the most experienced person when it comes to interpersonal relationships, but even I know that talking, sharing, becoming friends, involves a little bit of back and forth, a little bit of risk... But you don't like risk.'

Bo's chin jutted out. 'I can do risk.'

Remy snorted. 'In business—sure. Emotionally, you're a chicken.' She made herself smile at him, made herself pat his cheek even though her heart ached. 'A total wuss. And I suggest you deal with that—because I'd like the father of my children to teach them that life begins at the end of your comfort zone.'

Bo's eyes narrowed. 'I cannot *believe* that you have the gall to stand there and pass judgement on my choices, my life—especially since you're not exactly an expert in love and relationships. How many times have *you* been married? How many long-term relationships have *you* been in, huh?'

Such a valid point, Remy conceded, her heart aching.

'You can't just apply your big brain to matters of the heart, Remy! It doesn't work like that. We normal people don't operate like that...'

'"*We normal people...*"' Remy repeated his phrase. 'Like I haven't heard *that* all my life.'

She wanted to argue, but she knew that she couldn't.

'You're right—I have no idea what it feels like to love so intensely...' She hesitated, thinking that she, if she allowed herself, could fall into love like that. With him. *If* she allowed herself. Which she wouldn't. 'I don't know what it feels like to lose that kind of love, so I apologise. I was talking out of my hat.'

'Remy—'

Remy shook her head and darted out of the door. She couldn't be around him, keep talking to him, knowing that he thought she was a little strange…a lot exasperating. He might love her body, and he was already in love with his children, but he wasn't attracted to her mind.

Because he was 'normal' and she wasn't.

Thanks, life, for that latest reminder. FYI, it's not a lesson that I've ever been allowed to forget.

Bo took his shirt from the back of his athletic shorts and wiped the sweat off his face as he pounded down the road towards his house. When he'd slipped out the sun had been just dipping behind the horizon and pink shadows had slid across the vines. It was now nearly dark, and the evening air he was sucking in after a gruelling six miles was on the cold side of cool.

This was *his* time, his thinking time, but he couldn't get past the argument he'd just had with Remy. He'd hurt her with his 'normal people' comment and he regretted that. It had been said in the heat of temper but it was no excuse. His words had cut a lot deeper than he'd expected. And, recalling her telling him about her demanding mother, he supposed he could understand why. She'd never been allowed to be normal—she'd always been pushed to do more, *be* more.

'Normal' was what she'd been striving towards for years, and he'd slapped her down because she'd come a little too close to verbalising truths he'd prefer not to hear.

But was she right? *Was* he an emotional coward because he didn't want to risk loving someone, losing someone, again? Was that a bad thing? Wasn't he allowed to protect his heart, his soul, his emotions? He didn't want to go through the pain he'd experienced again—especially the pain of losing his wife.

Over the past few months he'd also started to realise that he couldn't ignore the last six months he spent with Ana and that he had to accept that his relationship with her hadn't been as perfect as he remembered it being. At the end some pretty serious cracks had developed, cracks he wasn't sure they would've been able to repair. Was he also scared of taking the risk of loving again and then it going wrong? Maybe. Probably. He had a right to avoid it. And if that meant being labelled a chicken, then he'd deal with it. Except that he didn't want his children living a half-existence, growing up to believe that love was scary, that it was painful. He wanted them to experience the joy of love and the profound happiness it brought them. Because he had felt that with Ana, ok, maybe not at the end but before that he'd been ecstatically happy. But how could he teach them that and still manage to protect himself?

On that point, was he as well protected as he thought he was? Remy had sneaked into the empty and guarded places of his heart and if something happened to her he would be devastated. He enjoyed her, cared for her, was constantly lusting over her, but that didn't necessarily mean that he was feeling more for her than he should. He couldn't be— *shouldn't* be. Falling for Remy would be stupid, crazy, terrifying. She was wilful and strong...but so vulnerable, and more in need of love than anyone he'd ever met.

Bo shook his head as he ran past Ginny's house. He had too much on his plate already, he thought, panicking. The business demanded so much from him and he was going to be a father in a couple of months. He couldn't afford to let this become any more complicated than it needed to be.

Remy was the mother of his kids and his temporary lover—his amazing but temporary lover. He had to keep it that simple. Because making it complicated by contemplating more was just asking life to bite him on the ass again.

It was late on Friday afternoon and Remy stood in the middle of the heaving supermarket, white fingers clutching the handle of her basket and quietly cursing. She knew she'd braved the madness of Friday afternoon shopping for a reason, but as soon as she'd stepped into the insanity her mind had gone absolutely, positively blank. Stamping her foot, Remy stared at the magnificent cheese display and tried to recall what could possibly have motivated her to be in this hellhole.

Her short-term memory loss—or baby brain—was worsening daily, Remy admitted wearily. Two days ago she'd asked Bo the same question twice, ten minutes apart, and he'd bluntly told her that she was losing it. She freely admitted that it was a very real possibility. She routinely lost the keys to the car, she'd found her hand cream in the fridge, and had quickly learnt to write down anything that was marginally important.

Twenty-four weeks down, sixteen to go—but because it was twins she'd probably only make twelve weeks before she went into labour. Her babies weren't just taking over her body: they were also affecting her mind. The father of her babies wasn't helping either. No, that wasn't fair, Remy admitted, staring at a pile of firebox-red peppers. Bo hadn't changed. He was still the same in-love-with-his-dead-wife man she'd met months ago—it was *her* feelings that had shifted, evolved.

Despite her best intentions she was falling in love with him; despite knowing that love was a crazy emotion that she wanted nothing to do with she was tumbling into that madness. And the more she tried to fight it, the deeper she fell. He was a spectacular human being: funny, smart, hot as hell. Loyal and passionate. She couldn't have chosen a better man to be the father of her children…

But while he was going to be in her life for a long, long time he would only ever be her temporary lover—and then they'd be, at best, friends and co-parents. As the mother of his children she would always have a place in his life, but it wasn't the one she most wanted—the one her restless and unhappy heart ached for.

She wanted to be his partner, his lover, the love of his life—but how could she compete with his dead wife? With a marriage that by all accounts had been made in the stars? Even if some miracle occurred and Bo decided that they *could* be more—have more, be a family—she knew that she would always be second-best, his second choice, the substitute mother and wife.

She'd always been the best, had always strived to be number one, and now she'd realised that most of her achievements, all the accolades for finishing first, meant nothing. But this race, for Bo's love, meant *everything*! And it was a race she could never win…not when her competition was a ghost.

Even if for some reason a miracle happened—which was highly unlikely—she'd always doubt his love, doubt that he loved her, wonder how much of his love was determined by the fact that she'd given him the family he'd always wanted. She'd always, always fall short of the mark…

She was an all or nothing type of girl…always had been.

She had to stop sleeping with him—had to find some distance from him. She had to retreat and shore up her defences, rebuild her walls. She was too close to falling over the edge…too close to handing over her heart and suggesting that he stamp on it. If she could remove herself from his orbit, put some space between them, then she could start working on how to manoeuvre him out of her heart and her head.

If she could fall in love with him, then with a little work and grace, and prayer, she could fall *out* of love with him too. Every action had an equal and opposite reaction. That was a universal law of science. Surely it could be applied to the human mind as well? Well, she was going to test the theory, and the first thing she needed to do was to move

out of his house, find her own place. She'd been trying to
find somewhere, but cottages and flats to rent were non-
existent. She'd just have to try harder—maybe look to
areas away from Bellevue.

Good plan, Remy thought as she headed for the exit,
tossing her basket into the pile on the way out.

As Remy passed the tables outside a busy coffee shop
a couple stood up from a table on the fringes and Remy
impulsively slid into a chair at the table, still warm from
the ample feminine bottom that was now waddling towards the parking lot.

Remy folded her arms on the table and pushed aside
the dirty coffee cups, sending the waitress a brief smile
as she hurried to remove the used crockery. After ordering a milkshake, she pulled a notebook out of her bag and
started to plan her retreat from Bo.

It would hurt, but not as much as allowing him to break
her heart over and over again if she was idiot enough to
hand it to him.

'Remy!'

Remy glanced up and smiled as Ginny weaved her way
through the tables towards her. Oh, this was wonderful!
She could do with Ginny's irreverent sense of humour, her
no-nonsense approach to life and her boundless support.
She could tell Ginny her memory-loss tales and know that
Ginny was laughing *with* her and not at her. Well, maybe
she'd laugh at her—but very kindly.

'Oh, you clever thing! Well done for getting a table—
and it's so *busy*! I thought we'd have to wait for ages.'

Remy accepted the kiss on her cheek and a quick hug.
Tucking her dress under her, she sighed internally at Ginny's slim-fit jeans and skimpy top. *She* wanted to wear sexy
jeans and skimpy tops. *She* wanted an even complexion
and bouncy hair—

Ginny turned to the side and draped one long leg over

her knee. She tapped an unvarnished nail on the small wooden table. 'What's the matter?'

Remy shrugged, embarrassed. 'I shot down here to buy something but I can't remember what. I stepped out of the car and—whoosh! Gone!'

'Hmm. So, do you think there's any chance that you might have come down here to meet *me*?' Ginny teased.

Remy groaned. 'When did we make this arrangement?'

'Three days ago.'

'I'm losing it. Seriously, Ginny, I need a brain transplant.'

'Well…' Ginny said, and then, seeing Remy's earnest worried face, she patted her hand. 'Everyone forgets things—especially in pregnancy.'

'You're being way too kind.'

'Your brain is just being stretched—and, God help you, you're living with my brother!' Ginny said gaily, and ordered two glasses of light wine and a massive slice of chocolate cake from a passing waiter. Seeing Remy's dubious expression, she snorted. 'It's a glass of low-alcohol wine—not one hundred per cent proof moonshine.'

'And the cake?'

'Scientifically proven to raise memory levels. And to raise serotonin levels—the happy hormone.'

'I have enough hormones in my system without adding another to the mix. Happy or not.' Remy propped her chin in her hand and fiddled with a small vase holding a perfect yellow daisy. 'I feel—I feel like I don't recognise myself. My driving sucks, your brother thinks I'm nuts, and I can't remember arrangements I make.'

And I'm determined to fall out of love with your brother because that was never part of the plan!

Remy felt her eyes well and frantically blinked away tears. She felt enough of a fool—she didn't need to be a blubbering one on top of it. She tossed her hair and managed a weak smile.

Ginny covered her hand with hers. 'What's going on, Rem?'

'I'm tired and weepy and emotional. Can we change the subject—' she looked up as the waitress placed the cake between them '—before I sob all over the cake?'

Ginny leaned forward and speared Remy with her amber eyes. 'No. I repeat: what's bugging you?'

'I'm fine.' Remy saw Ginny's eyes narrow and sulkily picked up her cake fork and stabbed the moist cake. 'Okay, I'm *not* fine. I'm living in Bo's house, off Bo's generosity.'

'He doesn't mind—'

'*I* mind, dammit! I don't *want* Bo's money!'

'Please, *please* don't tell me you want his love,' Ginny said equably, and daintily chewed a mouthful of rich, dark cake. Ginny scowled when Remy failed to deny her accusation. 'Dammit! I was worried this was going to happen.'

'I have just decided that I need to fall *out* of the little love I'm *in*,' Remy admitted reluctantly.

Ginny stared down at the table, and when she spoke again her voice was filled with regret. 'I think that's a great idea, Remy—not because I don't think that you're good for him, or because you don't deserve his love, but because I'm terrified that he buried all that with Ana and that he has none to give you. Or at least not what you deserve.' Ginny bit her bottom lip. 'He adored her, Remy— was besotted with her. I want that for *you* but I'm not sure he can love like that again…that he'll allow himself to love like that again. It's too big a risk for him.'

Yeah. She got that. God, what a mess.

'So you're saying that I should pull back emotionally?'

Ginny looked sad, but resolute. 'Yeah, I really do. Because I like you—hell, I *really* like you. And I want you to be happy. And being in love with a guy who can't love you the way you deserve to be loved is not fair on you.'

Ginny pushed her hair behind her ears and her expression turned hopeful.

'Maybe you aren't really in love with him? Maybe, for all your declarations of independence, you're doing what women throughout millennia do when they find themselves in a fix. They look for a mate. For a protector and a provider.'

Remy tipped her head and listened to Ginny's theory, ignoring the voice that insisted she was clutching at straws.

'Bo is for all intents and purposes what most women would consider a good catch. He's reasonably handsome—'

'Freaking hot...' Remy muttered.

Ginny grinned. 'He's financially fluid...has all his own teeth and hair. He's a perfect specimen and he's also the natural father of your babies.'

Remy let out a long sigh. She wished that Ginny was right—that the reason she felt warm and fuzzy every time Bo walked into the room was because she was terrified of walking this road alone. That because Bo refused to let her do that she was confusing her gratitude with love.

Oh, she wished it could be that easy.

But Ginny was looking so hopeful, so excited that she'd found an explanation for her craziness, that Remy couldn't disappoint her. 'Yeah, maybe that's it.'

Ginny smiled her relief but didn't get the chance to respond. Someone called out Ginny's name, and they both lifted their heads as a sleek blonde walked over to their table.

'Carina—hello. I didn't see you standing there! Carina, this is Remy, an old friend. Remy—Carina Westwood. She's an estate agent.'

Remy's ears pricked up. She liked meeting estate agents, and although it seemed as if she'd spoken to all the agents in the town, she hadn't got as far as Westwood's in the phone book to ask them whether they had any cottages to rent. None of the estate agents she had contacted so far had been able to find her a suitable two-bedroomed flat or cottage. It was deeply frustrating—

'How's business?' Ginny asked.

Carina readjusted the designer shoulder bag over her shoulder. 'Good. Rentals are a bit slow. I've got quite a few properties on my books—'

'Cottages?' Remy asked hopefully.

'One or two.' Carina's eyes widened as they fell on Remy's stomach and she grimaced. 'Oh, no—this is not happening.'

Remy laughed at her horrified face. 'It's not that bad. I'm just pregnant, and it's not contagious. Tell me, do you have any two-bedroomed properties?'

Carina's hand fluttered against her chest in agitation. 'Uh, no, I don't think so. Nothing that would suit you.'

Huh? What was going on? Remy clamped her tongue between her teeth before speaking, her tone very even. 'How would you know what might suit me?'

'Um…'

Remy narrowed her eyes. 'Why are you back-pedalling? You just said that rentals are slow, that you have proper-ties to rent, and I'm in the market. Sounds like a match made in heaven.'

'This can't be happening to me…' Carina muttered.

Something weird was going on here, Remy thought, pushing herself to her feet. 'I haven't been able to get a viewing on a single property to rent from any estate agents in the area in weeks. That sounds a bit screwy to me, since you have just confirmed that there *are* properties to rent. Now, would you like to tell me why you won't rent to me?'

'God, no!' Carina fluttered her hands in the air.

'Fine—I'll just report you to the estate agents board for

prejudicial behaviour. Maybe I'll write a letter to the local paper, stating the same complaint.'

A frown pulled Carina's super-thin eyebrows together. She shifted from foot to foot, uncertainty all over her face.

Remy held her stare, and Carina eventually let out a big sigh. 'Somebody from Bo Tessier's office called and strongly suggested that we don't rent to you.'

'What?' Remy kept her voice pitched low, but Carina was left in no doubt that her cup of anger was about to run over.

'Oh, dear...' Ginny murmured.

Carina threw up her hands. 'Okay, it was Bo's assistant. She said that if we ever wanted a chance to move any of the many properties the Belleaire Group owns, she suggested that we don't try too hard to find you a place to rent. No agent would risk losing out on a Belleaire sale for a small rental.' Carina's face fell. 'And since I've let the cat out of the bag, now I'll never get the chance to move *anything*.'

Ginny stood up and patted Carina on the shoulder. 'Relax—Bo is an idiot, but he's not unfair.'

'The sneaky, slimy, devious jerk!' Remy grabbed her bag off the corner of her chair and poked her finger into Carina's arm. Carina stepped back, her eyes widening, as Remy sent her her favourite corporate shark smile. 'You will set up a series of appointments for me to see *all* the cottages for rental in the area tomorrow. Are we clear?'

Carina swallowed and looked at Ginny for direction.

Ginny grinned widely. 'She's a lot scarier than Bo *and* she's pregnant. I'd listen, if I were you.'

Carina swallowed again, and together she and Ginny watched Remy waddle away. 'I am *so* screwed,' Carina wailed.

Ginny opened her wallet and withdrew some bills, tossing them onto the table with a flourish. 'Don't worry about it. *Bo*, however—' Ginny's eyes danced with glee '—stands to lose some *very* important parts of his anatomy. Feel sorry for *him*. He's toast.'

CHAPTER TEN

At Belleaire, Remy parked her truck in the visitors' parking area in the staff car parking and stomped her way up the path to the administration block of the Belleaire Group, which was screened from the tourist end of Belleaire by a thick copse of trees. This was her first visit to the office, and she followed the path to the tinted front door and yanked it open with such force that the pretty young receptionist jerked her head up.

'Ma'am, we're closed for the day,' she said, her high-pitched voice grating like nails on a chalkboard.

'Is Bo here?'

Pretty Young Thing found her gumption and lifted her nose in the air. 'Is he expecting you?'

'No—'

'Then I'm sorry. I cannot let you in without an appointment. His PA has already left for the day... Maybe you could call her and make an arrangement to see Mr Tessier?'

Remy slapped her hands on her hips and cocked her head. 'Call him and tell him that Remy is here.'

'No. As I said—'

To hell with this, Remy thought. She skirted the wide reception desk and headed straight for the door that led to the offices beyond.

'Hey, you can't go back there!'

'Just did.'

Remy lifted her hand in dismissal as she looked down the long passage. The area to her right seemed to hold a conference room, a kitchen and washroom facilities, so she headed down the passage, grateful for the nameplates on the doors. When she saw the sign for the CFO's office she knew she was getting closer. Then she ran out of passage, but directly in front of her was a door labelled 'PA to the CEO'.

Remy pushed it open and saw the door to Bo's office was open. Bo stood in front of the floor-to-ceiling windows, but instead of looking out at the view of the vineyards, and behind them the mountains, he was holding a large silver-framed photograph.

It could only be a picture of his wife—of Ana.

Perfect. Freaking perfect.

And wasn't that just another reason why she couldn't allow herself to feel anything more for this man than friendly detachment? Why she had to keep her emotional distance? She couldn't allow herself to think of him in any terms other than friendship because he certainly wasn't thinking of *her* in any other way.

He was still in love with his wife—he'd always be in love with his wife. She'd never be her, *couldn't* be her, and there was no way that she'd ever allow herself to feel as if she didn't quite live up to expectations.

She'd spent her entire life doing that, and she'd spent the last three years breaking that habit of a lifetime.

She wasn't going back there…not even for him.

Besides, maybe Ginny was right. Maybe she *was* just having a momentary loss of focus. Maybe she was letting her hormones rule, making her think that she needed a man to help and protect her. She could raise these children on her own if she had to. She didn't need Bo and she certainly didn't need Bo to love her to do it.

Love, she reminded herself, was a stupid, fickle emotion anyway.

Good talk, Remy, she said silently as she lightly rapped on the door.

Without waiting for him to tell her to come in, she walked into the room and slapped her hands on her hips.

'Did you genuinely think that you would get away with it?' she demanded, her eyes flashing gold fire.

Bo took his time replacing the frame on his credenza and Remy's eyes darted to the photo: blonde hair, blue eyes, unfairly gorgeous. *Enough of that,* she thought, and straightened her spine.

Bo placed his bottom on the corner of his desk and pulled down his tie. 'What are you talking about?'

'You put out a warning to the estate agents in the area "suggesting"—' Remy put air quotes around the word '—that they not rent a cottage to me.'

Bo's expression of cool assurance didn't change. 'So?'

'You had no right to do that!' Remy snapped as her temper started to bubble.

Bo lifted one powerful shoulder. 'I don't want you moving out of my place, and I especially don't want you living in town.'

Remy's fingers dug into her hips. 'I can't live with you for ever! At some point I am going to need my own place.'

Bo held the edges of his desk with a tight grip. 'I know that. I have a place for you to stay. The guest cottage— the house behind Eli's—is vacant. You can move in there when...' he looked down at her stomach '...when it's time.'

He had it all figured out, she thought, shaking her head at his take-control-and-do-it-my-way attitude. She doubted that the guest cottage would come with any type of rent or utility bills. Remy shook her head and strengthened her resolve. She'd been living with Bo for a couple of months now, but it was time to move on, to make him see that while she was, to an extent, willing for him to contribute financially and emotionally to raising their children, he was not responsible for her well-being.

Just rip the sticky plaster off, Remy. Quick and hard.

'That's not going to work for me,' she stated.

Bo straightened and his eyes deepened in colour—a sure sign that he wasn't happy. 'Excuse me?'

'Not going to work for me.' Remy repeated the words very slowly, as if she were talking to a deaf person.

As she'd expected, Bo's eyes deepened to the colour of wet slate. A muscle jumped in his jaw and Remy knew that, if she were clever, she'd back off...all the way off.

But that was what she'd done with her mother. She'd failed to stand up for herself. Never again. And if that meant taking on the devil, or Bo, then she'd do it.

'You don't get to make decisions for me, Bo. Ever. If I want to move into a cottage in town, or if I want to move to freaking Timbuktu, you can't and won't stop me.'

'I damn well *will*!' Bo growled. He was still in exactly the same position, but his entire body was vibrating with energy.

'I am not your wife—nor your girlfriend'

'You are the mother of my children!' Bo roared, running his hand through his hair.

'They are still inside *me*!' Remy shouted back. 'I am here—they are not! This is about me—not them.'

'This is about you being the most stubborn woman ever freaking created! Why are we fighting about this? I have a house—you need a house!'

'We're fighting about this because you didn't talk to me about moving to the guest house—you just decided that was what I should do!' Remy retaliated. She looked at the photograph and shook her head. 'Please tell me that your wife tolerated this macho alpha attitude!'

Remy knew that she'd crossed the line when his face

tightened and his eyes went from the heat of temper to the ice of pure anger.

'Leave Ana out of this. What we had together has *nothing* to do with you.'

'Of course it doesn't,' Remy mocked, pushing down the wave of hurt that had smacked her left of centre. 'You just wish that these were *her* kids, that she was here and I wasn't. I get it.'

Remy held up her hand as she saw him open his mouth to speak and shook her head.

'The problem is that I *am* here, these are my children, and you have to deal with it. And I'm not going to play the acquiescent woman, happy for you to orchestrate my life. Not going to happen. And the sooner you get used to that idea the easier this…this *situation* will be.'

Bo looked as if he had a lot to say, but Remy couldn't afford to listen. The tears were too close to the surface and any minute now the dam would break.

'I am *not* Ana. I will never be her. I will *not* be pushed around. I don't *need* you, Bo—do you understand that? I don't need your money. I can do this on my own! I don't need *anybody*!'

Bo cocked his head. 'Is that a threat?'

Yes…no—maybe. Probably. 'It's a statement.'

'Sounded like a threat to me.'

Bo stood up and walked across the room until he was standing so close to her that the tips of her breasts rubbed against his shirt front. Remy swallowed but refused to drop her eyes from his, not prepared to let him see that she was intimidated.

Because she was…just a little bit.

'Never,' Bo growled, his voice coated in ice, 'threaten to take my children away from me again. If we have a problem we sort it out—we yell and scream until we come to

a compromise—but we don't threaten. Ever. Don't do it again.'

Remy, feeling humiliated that her temper had pushed her into saying things she didn't actually mean, just looked mutinous.

Bo gripped her chin and squeezed. 'Are we clear?'

Remy narrowed her eyes. 'Only if you agree not to meddle in my business.'

Bo shook his head. 'When are you going to realise that you *are* my business? Now, get the hell out of my office. I have work to do.'

Remy shook her head. She wouldn't be so easily dismissed, wouldn't allow him to dictate her life, her actions, her future. *Just do it,* she told herself. *Take a deep breath and end it now...*

Remy put some steel into her spine and forced the words out. 'I'm calling it quits.'

Bo sent her a hot glare. 'What?'

Remy pointed her finger at his chest before pulling it back to herself. 'You and me. The affair... I'm ending it.'

'Why? Because I want you to live close to me?'

Remy wrapped her arms around her chest, suddenly feeling icy cold. Oh, God, this was going to be hard. Possibly the hardest thing she'd ever done. Maybe she was doing the wrong thing, going cold turkey; maybe there was another option...a middle ground. Maybe she *could* be part of his life, more than just the mother of his twins and his temporary lover. Maybe...

You're being a romantic fool, Remy told herself. *You're nothing more to him than an incubator and a willing body... This isn't a freakin' fairy tale. It's your life. So start dealing in what is!*

'You and I should never have complicated our lives by sleeping together. Sometimes I think that it would've been a lot easier if I'd left you out of this equation all together.'

Bo's face drained of colour. 'Do you really believe that?' he demanded, his voice low and taut.

Remy lifted a shoulder in a half-shrug. 'Yeah, I do. I wouldn't be second-guessing myself, having all these crazy feelings—wouldn't be constantly questioning my decisions. I wouldn't be competing with a gorgeous ghost. I wouldn't be feeling so…lost. Confused. Scared. I should've kept running.'

'I can't believe what you're saying.' Bo ground the words out. 'And, goddammit, if you think you're going to run now, I swear I'll hunt you down and bring you back. My children will be raised at Belleaire!'

Remy felt the bullet-like impact of his words and it took all her strength to keep her knees from buckling. It was one thing to suspect how he felt, but it hurt far more to have those fears confirmed. She *was* only of use to him as a willing body and an incubator. Whatever she'd thought he felt for her, any affection he had for her was only because she was useful to him. It was just another example of being appreciated for what she did and not for what she was…

But she'd never imagined that it would hurt this much. Maybe she was more deeply in love with him than she'd thought, than she was prepared to admit. His words had just ripped away all her obfuscation, the emotional smoke screen that she'd created between her feelings and the reality of her situation.

She was in love with him. But he saw her as a tool, as a way to achieve his objective. Any woman would have done—she wasn't anything special.

'God, I'm such a fool.' Remy looked at him with wide, helpless eyes. 'For someone who has an enormous brain, I am utterly stupid when it comes to men. Fantastically moronic when it comes to *you*.'

Bo frowned and pushed his hand through his hair. 'What the hell are you going on about?'

Remy released a little trill of pain-laced laughter. 'Oh, nothing serious! Just the fact that I feel so much more for you than you feel for me—that you see me as a plaything and an incubator for your chicks. Just that my heart is breaking because there is a walking, breathing woman in front of you who wants nothing more than to love you but you prefer to live in the past, where it's safe and secure, where you can't be hurt again. God, can I pick them or what? First my mother—then you. Why can't the people I love just love me back for what I am and not what I do?'

Bo just stared at her, looking as if he was trying to make sense of her words. 'I— What? You're in love with me?'

Idiot—of course she was.

She waved his comment away. 'That doesn't matter. What matters is that I'm walking away from this stupid situation. From Belleaire, from the bistro, from *you*. When the babies are born you can have visitation rights—supervised until I decide otherwise. You can pay child support—a reasonable sum—and I will take care of all the other bills. Other than that, I don't think we need to have much to do with each other.'

'I don't know what the hell is happening here!' Bo roared, temper flashing in his eyes.

Remy sent him a sad smile. 'Well, I'm leaving. So that'll give you some time to work it all out.'

Bo lifted his hand in entreaty. 'Remy—don't,' he said, his voice suddenly hoarse. 'Don't run away again. We can work this out.'

Remy walked over to the credenza, lifted the silver photo frame that contained Ana's picture and handed it to him. She lightly tapped the frame with her index finger and shook her head. 'No, Bo, we really can't.'

In the still, cold morning light, his hand fisted around the stems of a bunch of freesias, Bo started jogging up the path to the highest hill on the estate, to the small cemetery that held the ashes of all his family: his parents, his grandfather, Eli's mum. And Ana.

They were a couple of weeks off the fifth anniversary of her death, but Bo felt compelled to put some flowers on her grave, to try and connect with the memory of her.

He needed to spend some time with his best friend, his wife…

Except that there were a couple of problems with that statement. The biggest one being that it wasn't the truth any more. How could she still be his best friend and wife if she wasn't here? And for the last six months of her life they'd been at odds and he was no longer convinced that they would've survived her no-babies decree.

Remy was—had been, dammit—the one who'd listened to him talk after work, the one he'd held in his arms, the one he'd made love to at night and the one he'd be sharing a future with. Even if that future was only as the twins' father, as she'd insisted three weeks ago.

The longest three weeks of his life…

Bo jogged his way to the top of the path, and as he rounded the corner he saw the wooden bench he'd placed there years ago, overlooking Ana's memorial stone. Seeing the bench made his heart jump, and he dropped onto the wooden slats with a long sigh. Below him were the eastern situated vines and a series of tunnels growing organic fruit. Tall oak trees kept the cemetery in shade. Ana had once said it was the most peaceful spot on the estate, so he presumed she would have approved having her memorial stone right here.

Ana Hope Tessier
Death leaves a heartache no one can heal,
Love leaves a memory no one can steal.

'I still like the inscription.'

It was a measure of his tiredness that he didn't even flinch at the sound of Ana's voice inside his head.

'Ana, you're not real,' he muttered back.

'I thought you wanted to talk to me.'

Bo heard the amusement in Ana's ghostly voice and closed his eyes. He was going nuts. It was the only explanation.

'I need to talk—not to hear *you* talk.' Bo waited a beat. 'That's a lie. I do miss you.' He was partaking in this conversation…he definitely needed medical attention. But a part of him did still miss the marvellous relationship they'd shared for most of their time together.

'I know, but now you miss her too. So why are you here talking to me when you should be talking to her?'

He felt fingertips touch his shoulder and hurtled upwards, spinning in his seat. His heart slammed against his ribcage and he slumped into the corner of the bench. When he'd recovered his breath he scowled up at Ginny. 'You nearly gave me a freakin' heart attack!'

Ginny sat down next to him and pulled her feet up onto the bench. She smiled at him. 'Did you think I was a ghost?'

Bo wasn't going to dignify that with an answer—especially since it was partly true. 'Why are you here?' he demanded.

'Someone has to pull your head out of your ass,' Ginny replied, equable as ever. 'Why are you up here talking to Ana when you could be talking to Remy?'

'Not going there,' Bo warned her.

'You're sulking because, unlike Ana, she won't dance to your tune.'

Yeah; Ana had been easy-going except when it came to what was so incredibly important to him. He glanced at her stone and sighed. *Sorry, honey, but you know that's true.*

Bo brushed a hand across his forehead and scowled. 'Not. Going. There.'

'We so *are*,' Ginny assured him. 'Why won't you let yourself move on, Bo? You love Remy—any fool can see that.'

'I loved Ana,' he stated, a little desperately and knew his statement lacked the conviction he'd had half a year ago. 'I still love her.'

'Yeah? So? Why can't you love Remy too?'

That was what he was trying to work out.

Ginny expelled a frustrated sigh. 'You make everything so damn complicated, brother dear. You are *allowed* to love Remy too. You are man enough—have enough love—to do both. Ana is gone. Remy is here and I want you to be happy. She makes you so damn happy.'

'She does,' Bo admitted.

'Love her. Be happy. Think of Ana sometimes, but for God's sake live your life! You are using Ana as an excuse not to be with Remy, to not take a chance on love again, and she would *hate* that!'

Bo stared at the stone. Was that what he was doing? Was he clinging to Ana as an excuse so that he didn't have to risk feeling love? Being in love again? God, this felt weird, but it also felt like the truth. Maybe he *could* love Remy and still keep his promise to Ana. He was allowed to think of Ana, to miss her, but he could still laugh and love with Remy, could build a life with her.

With Remy... Even if she wasn't carrying his children...

The feelings he had for her were not tied up with the twins. They were distinctly separate. Yes, she was completely different from Ana—and that was okay. She was smart and stubborn and so damn vulnerable, thinking that she couldn't be loved for who she was. She was perfect, pregnant or not. Perfect for *him*...

'Be happy, darling.'

Bo felt a shimmer move through his hair. Was it Ana? Or was it just being so close to this place where he'd left her that made him imagine her voice? But if it was just his imagination why did he feel such peace? Why did he suddenly know exactly what to do and how to do it?

Bo slung his arm around Ginny's shoulders and kissed her head, before lifting his face to the weak autumn sunlight. 'Thanks, Gin.'

Thanks, Ana.

Remy gently pulled down the interior designer's rendition of what the Blue View Bistro would look like when it was completed and stared down at the paper in her hands. The walls were now painted those vibrant colours and the tables were mismatched, as was the crockery. There was exciting art on the walls and the terracotta floor sparkled. The kitchen had every appliance known to man and, more importantly, she'd trained the chefs to cook all the dishes on the menu she'd designed to perfection.

The staff the bistro needed had been hired and she could leave…she *should* leave. She had to leave because she was no longer *living*. She was only existing, Remy thought, folding up the piece of paper and tucking it into the back pocket of her jeans.

She walked out of her restaurant and quickly reminded herself that the restaurant wasn't hers. Nothing was, she thought as she pulled the door closed behind her.

She was now simply the woman who made the ten-minute drive from her rented cottage in town to Belleaire every day to her job as manager of the bistro, complete with a generous salary package. Oh, she was Ginny's friend, and Eli frequently arrived at midday to mooch lunch off her, but she hadn't had any real contact with Bo for more than twenty days.

The twice daily, early-morning and late at night 'Are you okay?' messages didn't really count.

As she walked towards her truck to go back to her empty cottage Remy reminded herself that he wasn't asking how she was—he was enquiring about the welfare of the twins... She knew that they were his top priority.

She still missed him, Remy thought as she drove back to her lonely little cottage on the outskirts of Bellevue. She missed his strong arms wrapped around her at night, his deep voice, missed feeling as if she was stronger and bolder and better when she was with him.

Remy used the back of her hand to wipe away the tear that clung to the tip of her nose and wondered when she'd stop crying over him.

She'd sent him an email earlier in the day, resigning as the manager-slash-chef of the Blue View. She couldn't work there any more. She couldn't cope with being so physically close to him, to seeing him in the distance but not being able to talk to him, laugh with him, love him. Besides, she was rapidly expanding, and the long days on her feet were taking a toll on her. She was mentally and physically whipped.

Until the babies were born she would sit at her desk in the cottage and take on the many consulting jobs that kept dropping into her inbox. They were brain-numbingly boring but they'd help pass the time. She wanted to meet her babies. She wanted to be so busy loving them, looking after them, that she forgot about the grey-eyed man who'd created them with her. They were the only thing she could imagine that might dislodge thoughts of him from her head.

Her mobile rang on the seat next to her and Remy glanced down at it before steering her truck to the side of the road and stopping. She scooped the phone up, sliding her thumb across the screen to answer the call. She didn't bother to hope that it would be Bo—he hadn't bothered to see her in weeks and she knew that he wouldn't. Bo was still in love with his wife and always would be…

'Remy, are you there?'

Remy sighed at her mother's voice in her ear and wished she'd checked to see who was calling before she'd answered. She really didn't feel like dealing with her mother's disappointment today.

'Hi.'

'You're still angry with me,' Jan stated, and Remy was surprised at her insight. Usually Jan didn't give much thought to what other people were thinking or feeling.

Remy started to deny her statement, then shrugged her shoulders and admitted the truth. 'Yeah, I am. I wasn't expecting you to support me, but I didn't expect such a violent reaction to the news that I am pregnant.'

'You took so long to tell me.'

'Why are you surprised by that? I knew that you wouldn't be happy,' Remy replied. 'Look, Mum, I'm tired and stressed, and I really don't want to fight with you. Can we postpone this argument?'

Jan didn't reply for the longest time, and after a tense few minutes Remy blew out her breath.

'Okay, well…good talking to you, Mum,' she said sarcastically. 'Bye—'

Remy tossed the phone onto the seat next to her and resumed driving. As she swung into the driveway in front of her tiny cottage her mobile rang again. God, how she wished she was back at Belleaire. But she didn't belong there any more. She didn't belong anywhere…

'What Mum?' Remy demanded.

'I was wrong,' Jan stated softly. 'About so much, and for far too long. You are so much more than your mind, Remy.'

Huh? What? This couldn't be her mother trying to apologise. Could it? 'Sorry?'

'I had no right to project my hopes and dreams on you, to try and live my life and unfulfilled ambitions through you,' Jan said firmly. 'And I never regretted having you—not once.'

Really? Remy climbed out of her truck and waddled towards her front door. Well, hell… What was she supposed to say to that? 'Um…okay?'

'I hope you can forgive me, and I promise never to mention computers again.'

That was a stretch. The corner of Remy's mouth kicked up. 'Never is long time, Mum.'

Jan's laugh was soft. 'Okay, I promise to try and not nag you. I'm just…really sorry, darling. I really am.'

Remy had never heard her mother apologise, so she knew that this was a watershed moment. She could either hold on to her resentment towards Jan or she could let it go. And, quite frankly, she had enough on her plate with a broken heart and rapidly approaching motherhood without borrowing more trouble.

'It's over, Mum,' Remy said, putting her key into the lock and twisting open her front door. 'We'll be fine.'

She heard Jan's sigh of relief as she stepped inside. She dropped her keys onto the hall table and frowned when her keys hit the tiled floor. Where was her table?

'What on earth…?' she murmured, looking around. Her cottage was empty—completely and utterly bare.

'What's the matter?' Jan demanded in her ear.

Remy was about to reply that she'd been robbed when she saw a sheet of paper in the middle of the floor of the empty living room. Even from a distance she could see the strong lines of Bo's handwriting and her heartbeat accelerated.

'I'll call you later, Mum.'

She shoved her mobile into her pocket and walked

across the room. She stood over the piece of paper and read the words written below.

Your stuff has been kidnapped. The ransom is dinner, my place, tonight, six o'clock. We'll discuss whether you get it back then.

Remy, furious, yanked her mobile out of her pocket and angrily punched in his number. He answered immediately.

'Robert Tessier, what the *hell* have you done with my things?'

'What did my note say?' he replied genially.

She glanced down. 'That the price of getting my stuff back is dinner tonight. Your place at six.'

'Well, don't be late.'

'You *stole* the furniture, Tessier. It's not mine! I rented this place furnished! You could be arrested, you know! In fact, I think I'm going to report that I've been burgled.'

'Don't bother,' Bo said lazily. 'I got the owner's permission to temporarily abscond with his furniture.'

'This is nuts. *You* are nuts.'

'Tick-tock, babe.'

Remy hurried across the cottage, stormed into her bedroom and, despite knowing that they would be empty, yanked open the cupboard doors. 'I'm filthy and tired and I want to shower and change. You also stole all my clothes!'

'So come naked. Trust me, I won't complain.'

The grin she heard in his voice locked her jaw.

'You are the most arrogant, managing, annoying—'

Bo broke into her rant. 'Be here at six or you'll never see your stuff again.'

Remy stared at her dead phone. Seriously?

She knocked on his front door a half-hour late, just as he'd expected her to, and he knew that she'd used that time to stoke her temper. She looked like a fluffed up bantam hen—annoyed and flustered.

He'd never loved her more.

Remy stepped inside his house and tapped her foot in aggravation. 'So, what's this about?'

'Lots of things,' Bo replied, pulling her into his house and closing the door behind her.

It had started to drizzle outside and the thought of her driving on a wet road made his heart clench. She wasn't Ana, he reminded himself. Nothing was going to happen to her.

He pulled in a deep breath and resisted the urge to pull her into his arms. If he did, he'd lose her before he even started. Remy, unfortunately, would not be placated by a couple of hot kisses.

Pity, because it would be so much easier than eating crow.

'Do you want some wine?' he asked. 'Maybe a half-glass?' He gestured to an open bottle of fifteen-year-old Merlot standing next to two glasses on the coffee table in his lounge.

'No. I'd like my stuff back—and maybe an explanation for your craziness,' Remy stated, her gold eyes flashing fire. 'You haven't spoken to me for three weeks and then you do *this*? What the hell are you thinking?'

'I did text you. I was worried about you.'

'*Pfft*. You were worried about the twins—not me,' Remy replied quickly, and he saw the pain in her eyes before she whirled away to stomp over to the window to stare out into the darkness.

He'd really messed this up, Bo thought, angry at himself. She really believed that her only worth to him was the fact that she was carrying his children. He'd hurt her, and by not contacting her he'd allowed her to keep believing that. He rubbed his hand over his rough jaw and felt thoroughly ashamed of himself.

Bo walked up to her and stood behind her, as close as he could without touching her. He felt her tense and lightly rested his hand on her hip. 'No, don't move…just listen,' he said when she started to move away. 'When I texted you I was asking about *you*—how *you* were. I've spent every minute of the past few weeks worrying about you.'

'Yeah, right…' Remy muttered.

Okay, he didn't blame her for not believing him, but he could show her. He intended to—soon.

Remy dropped her head to stare at the floor. 'Just give me my stuff back and let me go, Bo. This isn't helping.'

Bo turned her around and lifted her chin to make her look at him. His heart clenched at the tears brimming in her eyes. 'This is about your stuff being in the right place and getting you to follow.'

'You're not making any sense,' Remy complained. 'And you have a very peculiar expression on your face.'

Bo shrugged, slightly embarrassed. 'I'm trying to tell you that I love you. For the past few months I've loved you in different ways at different times, but today I realised that I just *love* you. In every way possible.'

He saw hope flare in her eyes, but then it died just as rapidly as it had appeared.

'You don't love me—and even if you do, it's just rubbing off because you love our children so damn much.'

A tear fell and his heart broke just a little.

'You don't love me anything like you love Ana.'

Bo stroked her bottom lip with his thumb. 'And you call *me* stubborn?' He shook his head and picked up her hand. 'Come with me.'

He loved her? Was that really what he'd said? *What?* For the first time in her life Remy couldn't think straight, couldn't think of anything but what he'd said…

I just love you. In every way possible.

Oh, how she wanted to believe him.

His hand was tight around hers, but when Remy saw where he was taking her she planted her feet and shook her head. She was *not* going into Ana's room—not again. She was not going to compete with a ghost and lose to a ghost... *Been there, hated that.*

She tried to tug her hand from Bo's grip but he held her tight. 'Let me go, Bo, please. I can't do this.'

'Yeah, you can. I need you to come inside with me. Trust me, Rem—please?' Bo said calmly. 'Give me a chance to explain, to put this behind us.'

She wanted to walk away, to keep her heart protected, but she couldn't resist the entreaty on his face. His eyes were steady and she hadn't seen those shutters fall once.

Bo used his other hand to open the door and Remy looked past him into the bedroom. The first thing she noticed was that the massive portrait of Ana was gone from above his bed...along with the bed and all the other furniture. Even the curtains were gone.

Remy stepped into the room and lifted her hands in confusion. 'What is it with you and bare rooms today?'

'I'm trying to make a point.' Bo leaned his shoulder into the door frame and lifted his mouth into a semi-smile. 'Ana and I only moved into this house a month before she died—did you know that?'

How would she know that since he never spoke about her?' 'No.'

'So, in reality, this isn't really her house. It's mine.'

Remy really didn't know where he was going with this. 'I'm not following you.'

'I love this house, and I'd like to carry on living here— with you. I want to share this room with you, so I stripped it.'

Remy blinked, trying to assimilate everything he was saying.

'And if you think that you might be able to live here with me, I want you to choose what goes back in this bedroom. I want this room to be our room, this house to be our home, the twins' home.'

'Uh…'

Bo ran a frustrated hand over his face. 'I'll strip the whole damn house, if that's what you need. I'll build another house, if that's what makes you feel comfortable. Hell, I'll even move into that stupid rabbit hutch you've been living in lately if that makes you happy. I just want to be with you.'

Remy looked at his emotion-filled eyes and bit her bottom lip. It would be so easy to throw herself into his arms, to surrender to the happiness that wanted to consume her, but she couldn't—not just yet. She had to be sensible…

So she stepped away from him and paced to the windows and back, wringing her hands. 'Look, Bo, I appreciate the sentiment and the gesture…'

'But…?'

'But I know that you are an intensely loyal person and that you have loved Ana for a long, long time. You say you love me now, but I don't know if you are going to change your mind again. I don't know if you love me because you want a family and this is your way to get one. I need to know that you love me for *me*. I don't want to compete with a ghost and I don't want to get hurt again. I don't know if my…' She stuttered to a stop and then forced the words out. 'If my heart can stand it.'

Bo looked at her and folded his arms. He nodded once and cocked his head. After a long silence he started to speak. 'I can't make you believe me, Rem. All I can do is tell you that I love you and that my love for you is completely and utterly separate from my love for our children. I would be begging you to love me, be with me, even if you weren't round and lovely and carrying my sons.'

'Daughters.' Remy automatically contradicted him.

Bo smiled as he walked over to her and cupped her face in his big hands. 'I loved Ana deeply, Rem. I'm not going to deny that. But I loved her when she alive and I was a different man. I've moved on, and you're here, and it's *you* that I'm utterly crazy about. You are the first thought in my head when I wake up and the last thing on my mind when I go to sleep...*you*, Remy. I love you—please believe me. Give me another chance to prove it to you.'

Remy blinked her astonishment. She was standing in an empty room, her face and her heart in the hands of this amazing man, and she was *hesitating*? What was wrong with her? She had a second chance to be happy and by God she was taking it!

She leaned back and smiled at him, suddenly totally at peace. This was how it should be, she thought. All she'd needed was this simple, sincere declaration from him and her world made complete sense.

Bo's love didn't need fanfare and parades: it was quietly deep. His love was reflected in his actions and Remy had absolutely no doubt that she would always come first in his life.

She took a deep breath and blurted out her next words. 'So when do you want to get married?'

To his credit, Bo didn't even flinch. He just brushed his lips across hers and smiled. 'Oh, so *now* you want to get married?'

Remy sent him a teasing look. 'The twins might not appreciate being illegitimate.'

Strong arms pulled her towards him. 'Not a good enough reason to get married. Give me another one,' he commanded.

Remy lifted her hand to touch his cheek. 'I love you. I want to be your wife. Is that okay?'

Bo's eyes went soft. 'That's very okay.'

Bo's mouth touched hers and Remy sighed. This was where she belonged, she thought. This was what she'd been looking for: this man, this place, this life. Standing there, in his empty bedroom, she kissed him as her hands travelled up and down his body, so grateful that she was back in his arms and back in his life.

After long, love-soaked minutes she lifted her mouth from his and placed her hands on his chest. His hands were down the back of her panties and warm on her bare flesh.

'Please tell me that the guest bedroom still has a bed?' she asked with a cocked eyebrow.

Bo bent down and scooped her off her feet, held her against his chest. 'It most definitely does. Let me show you.' Then he stopped and looked down at her, love and happiness making him look younger. 'Just promise me that you won't fall asleep midway through, okay?'

Remy grinned. 'Make it good, then.'

'Oh, I intend to. Every day for the rest of our lives, Rem.'

Now, *there* was a promise she could believe in, Remy thought as he carried her off to start the rest of their lives.

EPILOGUE

Two years later

A NEW 4D model sat on Dr Graham's desk and Bo couldn't help noticing that his wife refused to look at it. She'd refused to look at anything since she'd found out that he'd made an appointment with Henry and insisted that she have a physical.

It was all her fault for being so stubborn and refusing to consider the obvious.

'I am *not* pregnant,' she told him for the hundredth time, and he just smiled at her.

God, he loved her. He reached across, took her hand and pulled it across so that it rested on his thigh. 'So you keep telling me. But if you'd been prepared to do a test, like I asked, you wouldn't be here.'

'I am *not* pregnant,' Remy insisted, her eyes huge in her face.

She was. Of course she was. He could tell—he knew her that well. 'Would it be such a bad thing if you were, Rem?' he asked gently.

Remy rested her head on his shoulder and closed her eyes. 'Of course not… But I don't have time to be pregnant, Bo! We're expanding the Little Blue and opening the new restaurant in Calistoga. The online deli and wine shop is so *busy* and our boys run me ragged. And I sort of thought that two was it…?'

Bo just shrugged. He'd have a football team if she'd co-operate.

'Besides, I'm on the pill. There has to be another reason I'm late.'

Remy tried to glare at him but, as always, he saw the love in her eyes.

'And if I am, then it's you and your super-sperms' fault.'

Bo smiled at her machine-gun conversation. A nervous Remy was a voluble Remy, and she had yet to shut up this morning.

'Can I phone the twins?' Remy pleaded, tugging on his hand.

'No. You spoke to them fifteen minutes ago and they're fine. Ginny is spoiling them rotten on their first sleepover.'

'They're only fifteen months old!' Remy protested. 'Too young to be sleeping out of their own beds.'

She might think so, but their sons had been born hell-raisers and Bo had no doubt that they had Ginny sussed already. They were pure, undiluted energy without an off switch, bright, funny and insatiably curious, and Bo knew that they were going to keep them on their toes.

Bring it on, he thought on a grin. He couldn't wait.

He had these two wonderful boys in his life because of this amazing woman, whom he loved with every strand of DNA he had. She was his everything….

Henry Graham stepped into the room and after shaking hands with them both placed his hands on his hips. 'So…pregnant again?'

'I don't think so—he does,' Remy stated, jerking a thumb in his direction.

Henry smiled and nodded his head towards the sonar machine. 'Well, we can either do a quick pregnancy test or a quick scan. If the test shows up positive, then I'll do a scan anyway, so why don't we skip that step and you hop onto the bed and let me take a look?'

Bo felt his heartbeat accelerate as Remy lay down on the bed and unzipped her linen trousers to expose her tummy. Her body was slim and long and he loved it, but he couldn't help feel excited at thought of her blooming with life again.

Henry squirted gel onto her stomach, then placed the probe and started moving it around. Bo felt her hand sneak into his and dropped a quick kiss on her lips.

'Love you,' he stated quietly.

'Love you back,' Remy whispered, and looked towards the screen.

'Well, Bo is right, Remy—you are definitely pregnant. There's the amniotic sac and there's the heartbeat… No, wait…there's *two* heartbeats!' Henry said, laughter in his voice.

Bo sent him a quick look and Henry shook his head. He watched Remy as the words sank in. Her eyes looked shocked.

'Uh…*gumf*…*whaaat*? I'm actually *pregnant*? With *more twins*?'

Over her head, he and Henry exchanged conspiratorial grins. Then they heard Remy's shallow breathing.

'She's looking rather white and like she might faint. Maybe you should put her out of her misery, Bo?' Henry suggested.

Bo leaned over her and cupped her face in his hands. 'Breathe, darling. That's a joke—we're not having twins,' he told her.

She almost looked disappointed and he could relate to that.

'We're *not*?'

'But, like I repeatedly told you, we *are* having another baby.'

Remy looked at the screen and back at him, and he held his breath, waiting for her reaction. His heart resumed beating when she smiled.

'This time it had better be a girl,' she told him, her eyes finally filling with excitement. 'There's far too much testosterone in our house as it is!'

Bo rested his forehead against hers. 'And we all love you wildly.'

Remy smiled and touched his lips with hers. 'You really do.' She whispered against his mouth. 'I'm a very lucky girl.'

* * * * *

MILLS & BOON®
MODERN™

POWER, PASSION AND IRRESISTIBLE TEMPTATION

A sneak peek at next month's titles...

In stores from 17th July 2015:

- **The Greek Demands His Heir** – Lynne Graham
- **His Sicilian Cinderella** – Carol Marinelli
- **The Perfect Cazorla Wife** – Michelle Smart
- **The Marakaios Baby** – Kate Hewitt

In stores from 7th August 2015:

- **The Sinner's Marriage Redemption** – Annie West
- **Captivated by the Greek** – Julia James
- **Claimed for His Duty** – Tara Pammi
- **The Playboy of Argentina** – Bella Frances

Available at WHSmith, Tesco, Asda, Eason, Amazon and Apple

Just can't wait?
Buy our books online a month before they hit the shops!
visit www.millsandboon.co.uk

These books are also available in eBook format!

0715/01